WARS END

THE HALF-BREED GUNSLINGER V

BRET LEE HART

Wars End
   The Half-Breed Gunslinger V
Copyright 2018, 2022 Bret Lee Hart
ISBN-13: 9798825773698
Cover Art Copyright 2022 Laura Shinn Designs
http://laurashinn.yolasite.com
(Revised cover & formatting, 2022)

WARS END
The Half-Breed Gunslinger V

The three year Montgomery/ Dolin War was over, and not one family member named Montgomery was left alive. Hunter James Dolin had killed Richard Montgomery, his brother Duke Montgomery and their sister Jane Montgomery. The next man in line named Little Owl, for Chief of the Snake Clan of the Miccosukee, of the Seminole Indian Tribe was killed by the hand of the Half-Breed Gunslinger. Little Owl and his loyal braves were no more.

Myakka City and the James family had survived the last battle and Helen and little James were found alive at the waters' edge. Their current enemies were dead but Hunter was concerned about the wanted posters. There was no way to know how many had been printed and how far they had spread? The authors of the prints were dead but it would take time for this to be known and then believed. Five thousand dollars was a world of money and there would be men coming to kill the Half-breed Gunslinger and seeking their fortune.

CHAPTER ONE

Helen and little James had come very close to drowning in the rushing river. Only a mother's love and determination to survive willed her the strength to save her child. They were exhausted and hungry in need of rest and may have died under the big oak if Hunter had not found them when he did. The night was falling and along with it the temperature. This time of year the nights in the swamp could bring a chill and on top of their wet cloths and tired bodies sickness could take hold.

They would spend the night under the tree and move on at first light. Hunter gathered wood and prepared a fire. They ate jerky and warmed their insides with coffee. Helen and little James turned over every so often next to the fire to dry their cloths and soon they felt much improved.

Helen and little James slept; Hunter did not. He would keep watch through the night. They had wandered onto cattle baron land and their trespass could bring danger. The Indians were still a concern; Hunter had killed the Chief of the Seminole tribe of the Snake clan and with him many of the clan's warriors. There was no telling how the rest of the Miccosukee would react to the death of Little Owl. If the wise mother of the tribe, Alameda, was accepted as ruler they would most likely be given passage, but sooner or later a male warrior brave must take her place as Chief of the Snake Clan.

The sun crept up but was not seen for the gloomy day would not allow it. Overcast and dampness was the start of the morning as a cold front blew through from the north. The air was unusually dry for the swamp but it would not last as the southern winds would push back by the afternoon.

Hunter had saddled the horses and while Helen and little James still slept, he was ready to move on. He looked down on them with concern. They needed days of rest in a warm bed with herb laden soup. The Seminole village was three days ride to the North, there was nothing but swamp to the south, and to the east and the west Hunter did not know. There weren't any towns this far south only homesteads spread out, owned by ranchers and locals who were not always friendly. He had not seen any fencing or signs but the cattle he had seen grazing verified he was on cattle baron land, these cattle men where called open-rangers. Hunter must make a decision; a three day horse ride back to the Snake clan or seek out the cracker ranchers and hope that they were honorable and friendly. As he pondered this his decision was suddenly made for him, when the sounds of thundering hooves could be heard off in the distance. As the sounds got closer he could make out four to five horses moving fast toward them. Hunters Appaloosa named Zeke and Helens mayor named lady were soon on alert; their ears had perked up at the same moment that Hunter had turned his head looking up the hill past where the cattle grazed. Hunter removed his buckskin jacket and began walking forward. They were heading directly for him and the big oak where Helen and the child lay sleeping. He wanted to get between the horseman and his family and he did so carefully judging the distance, stopping at a place where he could get back and protect them. As they approached,

Hunter took the gunslingers stance prepared to shoot it out, to the death if need be.

They lined up their horses in front of the gunslinger, side by side in a row. They were hard men; Gunmen and cattle men rolled up into one, no telling which had come first. The large elder man with an impressive graying beard and leading the way was clearly the cattle baron, the boss whose orders would be carried out without question. He was the first to speak,

"I am Captain William B. Hooker, and you're trespassin' on Hooker land."

"I ask for safe passage for this woman and child who are in need of medical care." Hunter moved his head toward the tree but he did not take his eyes from the men on horseback. "We had a run in with some renegade Seminoles, the woman and child ended up bein' washed down river and landed here, tresspassin' was not our intent."

"Must- a -bin Little Owl Captain," said one of the drovers, "that one has been nothin' but trouble round here lately."

"How-d you git through it son, asked the Captain, "Little owl don't give up on a pursuit lightly."

"I killed Little Owl and many of his braves."

"You sayin' you kilt your own kind," the same drover who spoke before asked while repositioning his self in the saddle. "You is half-breed right?"

"Daryl, shut up." The Captain demanded. "The sheer matter they're alive proves it to be somewhat true."

There was a long pause and Hunter knew a decision was being made.

"Daryl, fetch the wagon."

Hunter loosened up just a little.

"Mr...?" asked The Captain.

"Dolin"

"Mr. Dolin, the ranch house ain't far from here, and you're in luck, the Doc were called in for one a' my boys. He should be arriving soon."

"I'd be in your debt." Hunter said with a tip of his hat.

Helen and little James rode in the back of the wagon. Hunter followed on Zeke with Lady in tow to the ranch house. They traveled only three quarters of a mile to the impressive but modest wood structure that stood on the top of a slight hill. It was single story but long and wide. The barn was half the length but twice the height; this was typical on a cattle ranch. Every cracker carried a whip and the cows were the center of everything, they were the food, the product of the wealth and the meaning behind a cracker cowboy's whole existence. The only things as important as the cattle were the horses and the guns that the men carried to protect the herd.

In Hunters mind he recalled this Captain William B. Hooker. The man was well known throughout Florida. In his younger years he was a lawman and then a soldier who fought in the Seminole Indian wars. This concerned Hunter because he himself was an outlaw and part Indian, two marks against him with a man like Hooker.

They put up Helen and the child in a guest room on the first floor in the main house. It was warm and dry and the bed was fancy like Hunter had never seen. Helen and little James had soup and milk while tucked in bed and Hunter drank soup from a metal tin cup. The woman and child would need at least a day's rest before moving on.

Hunter was sitting in a wood chair at the side of the bed but stood quickly when Doc Holt walked into the room.

"Well I'll be damned!" exclaimed the Doc when he saw the gunslinger. "You got more lives than a cat young man."

"Lucky I guess?"

"Beatin' the infection ain't no little thing son."

Doc grabbed Hunters chair and slid it to the bed side. His focus was totally on his patients now as if Hunter was not in the room any longer.

Helen's eyes opened and she smiled when she saw the old man.

"Doc Holt, what a pleasant surprise, how are you."

"How are you is the question little lady."

The Doc pulled a stethoscope made of cedar from a wood box and put it to Helens chest and listened. He then put it to the chest of little James.

"What are you feeling in the chest area?"

"I am fine, I am just tired."

"Did you take-in much water?" The Doc asked as he put his ear to the stethoscope and the other end on her chest once again.

"I took in some as I tried to keep James above the water line."

"Take a deep breath please."

Helen sucked in air and then began to cough. The doc put the scope on little James chest. The boy was now awake and his big eyes were staring at the old man with question.

"Can you breathe deep for me son?"

James looked at his mother who had finished her coughing fit.

"Go ahead, honey, it's ok." She assured him.

The child took a deep breath, and then again.

"The boy is clear," said the doc, "but you little lady have some fluid in the lungs."

"Will I be okay, doc?"

He put his hand on her head as he spoke.

"You're not runnin' a fever, two days rest and you'll be fine I think. Warm meals and hot tea and when you're ready to move on," the doc bent down and opened another smaller wood case and pulled out a small glass vile, "mix this with water, beer or tea for you and the boy."

"What is it Doc?" Helen asked.

"Coca wine, for fatigue of mind and body, it will give you the energy for your trip, it's the newest thing. How do you think at my age I get around so good?"

Doc Holt said his short goodbyes and left the room while muttering about his next stop. His boot stomps could be heard walking down the hall, a door opened and then slammed shut. Hunter went to the window where he saw Captain Hooker pay the Doc in silver. The wagon rattled and creaked as the Doc snapped the reigns and put the horse into motion and riding on. *There goes the only witness*, thought Hunter.

After a time Helen and little James was sound asleep. Hunter decided he would check on the horses and left the room, closing the door quietly. He walked the hall to the open foyer by the front doors and was met by Hooker and four men with their guns drawn.

"What the hell is this captain?"

"Hunter James Dolin wanted for murder, that's what this is."

"Five thousand dollars to boot." said the drover, the same drover with the big mouth at the tree. *Daryl*, thought Hunter, he would not forget this man's name again.

"You drop them guns and come peaceful like and the woman and the boy will be escorted home safe and sound. I give my word as Captain William B. Hooker."

"Your word," Hunter replied, "why should I take your word?"

"You ain't got no choice half-breed." sneered Daryl.

"Daryl, shut up!" demanded Hooker. He then turned his attention back to Hunter. "You know of me gunslinger, and I know of you. We either shoot it out right here and now or you hand over them pistols, your choice."

It was five against one; Hunter knew he could get a bullet in each man but their guns were drawn and the hammers were cocked. The area was too small for him to avoid their bullets and he would surely take some led. If it weren't for Helen and the boy he would have already drawn, but he had to think of them first.

Hunter slowly un-buckled his gun belt and let it drop to the floor. He then raised his hands slightly. Daryl stepped in after a nod from Hooker and pulled the shotgun from Hunters side holster. He did it with a grin that Hunter swore to wipe of his face permanently at the first opportunity.

"The knife." said Hooker.

Hunter reached back and pulled the Bowie from the sheath that was clipped to his pants at his back. Daryl took that to, with the same grin only bigger.

"You take good care of that Daryl; I will be needin' that back."

The stare of the gunslingers steel blue eyes froze Daryl for a moment. His smile faded and then came back but only a little.

"Oh you won't need this no more Half-breed, not where you goin'"

"Daryl! I'm only gonna tell yah one more time to shut the hell up." The Captain warned. "Jimbo, tie his hands in the front, he's got to ride."

The big mouth drover picked up Hunters pistol belt from the floor as Jimbo escorted the gunslinger outside. Zeke was there, and Hunter was placed on his back by two of the men.

"Where we headed Captain?" Hunter asked.

"Daryl and Jimbo here will take you to Fort Foster and we'll let the army decide your fate."

"What of my family Captain?" Hunter asked.

"When they are ready for travel I will personally escort them where ever they would like to go, un-harmed, I give you my word as a lawman and a gentleman."

"You do as you say Captain and I will allow you to live, I give you my word, but your men here, a pass will not be givin'."

Jimbo glared at Hunter and Daryl laughed out loud.

"Let's go tough guy." Jimbo replied.

"You try anythin' half-breed and I'll kill yah with your own guns." Daryl said this while resting his hand on Hunters 44's that he now wore on his hip. Hunter was glad to see his Bowie knife tucked in the man's belt for he would need it as well on his return. Hunter spotted the double barrel shotgun which hung in its holster strapped to the side of Jimbo's horse.

CHAPTER TWO

Two weeks had passed since the gunslinger and Helen had left to rescue their child in the Seminole Indian Lands. Jebidiah and Walt were sitting at the table in the back foyer of the hotel discussing what should be done when Bodie and Bird walked in; Walt poured them a drink as they sat while Jebidiah began to pace.

"It's been fifteen days with no news and I ain't sure what we should do?"

"Easy simmer Jeb," said Walt, "It's a three or four days ride one way, they ain't for sure overdue just yet."

Bodie spoke up from his seat, "Me and Bird here can go fetch um, just say the word."

"Them crackers will be comin' through town here in a day or two on their return cattle drive," spouted Walt, "and we need you 'all here to help keep the peace, me and Jeb are gittin' too old for this sh…"

Jebidiah interrupted Walt before he could finish his speech for he had heard it a thousand times before. "Look I'm worried, we need to do somthin'."

"It's been what, two weeks?" asked Walt, "when it's twice that then we'll do somethin'and I will personally lead the way. Why am I suddenly a voice of reason here? Hell must be gitten' ready to freezin' over?"

Bird had said nothing to this point and Bodie suddenly noticed the boy was fidgeting.

"What do you think Birdie boy?" Bodie asked.

"You all want to know what I think?" asked Bird.

"I wouldn't be puttin' a question to ya if I didn't. replied Bodie.

They were all gazing at Bird and then Walt put his arms out and shook his head impatiently.

"I think we have another problem that needs attention." Bird stopped there and bowed his head.

"Well spit it out boy before the day passes." said Walt.

"The dogs missin.'"

"Missin'!" exclaimed Bodie, "what do you mean missin.'?"

"I been feddin' and playin' with her every day, hell I even washed her, and this mornin' she was just gone. I found her tracks..."

"Let me guess," Said Jebidiah, "Mocha's headin' straight in the direction for the Gunslinger, Helen and little James?"

Bird nodded his head in agreement, "I got to go after her, and she was in my charge."

"Well that settles that," Bodie replied, "let's pack it up Bird, I'm goin' with yah." He then directed his talk to Jebidiah and Walt. "you two are just gonna' have to handle them cracker cowboys 'round here without us."

Jebidiah agreed with a look of relief, for he had a bad feeling that the Gunslinger, Helen and the boy had found trouble, and now Mocha?

"I think you all are jumpin' the gun just a bit, "said Walt, "but now that the dog is gone missin'..."

Walt gave Bird a stare that made the boy cringe. He wanted to tell the old coot off but he knew Walt was right in his accusation. Mocha had been his responsibility. Bodie stood and palmed Bird on the back trying to reassure the boy.

"Now that I think on it Walt," said Bodie, "I know a couple a' Okeechobee boys that are good with a gun, for a bar tab they would give you and Jeb a hand here in town, maybe?"

"A bar tab? You mean free liquor?" asked Walt.

"Yes Walt, they are brothers and they do like to pull a cork, but they will do as they are told. There good ole boys that's all."

Before Walt could argue Jebidiah jumped in and cut him off.

"Agreed, you should leave at once."

"Let's git it boy," said Bodie, "we'll stop on the way and talk with Boomer and Billy McCaw, you'll know within a day or two what is their answer."

Bodie and Bird headed south following Mocha's tracks. They were loaded for bear but hunting a dog, Mocha would lead them to Hunter, Helen and the child.

CHAPTER THREE

Fort Foster was ten days away at the speed the men were traveling. Jimbo was a Texas man and the smarter of the two; Daryl was a Kentucky boy who drank constantly. Hunter knew he could sneak away in the night unseen if he wished. The two men would never find him in the swamps but he wanted his horse, guns and the Bowie knife. Hunter would wait for the right opportunity; and that opportunity would include getting his hands on the big mouth Kentucky boy named Daryl.

The third night out Jimbo cooked steaks on a fire. Meat butchered from the cows at Hookers ranch. The sizzling sounds and smell from the beef made a man's mouth water. The best part of working a cattle ranch was you always ate well.

Jimbo plated a steak and Daryl brought it over to the gunslinger were he sat against a downed log, ten feet from the fire. Hunter's hands were tied in the front with rawhide given him about eight inches of slack at the wrist. No one seemed to have noticed that the tips of Hunters boots were razor sharp, for all the traveling dirt had covered the shiny metal. He could easily cut the leather strap that bound him, but he was waiting for the right time.

Daryl spat on the steak before he handed it over, Hunter took it and stared the man down with his steel blue eyes.

"Sorry 'bout that Half-breed, got a little cold workin' here." Daryl's grin showed rotting teeth.

"Knock it off Daryl," scolded Jimbo, "we got a job to do, no need to make it more difficult."

"You gonna hand me that knife so I can cut this up?" Hunter asked nodding at his Bowie in Daryl's belt.

"Na, you got good teeth for tarrin' meat, we don't give sharp objects to savages."

Hunter ate his meat like a sandwich, avoiding the area where Daryl had spat. He watched his captors eat there plated steak by the fire. They were both drinking whiskey; Daryl was hitting it particularly hard tonight. Jimbo stood and walked over to Hunters side and tipped the bottle for him, Hunter drank.

"Don't be givin' him the whiskey!" Protested Daryl "you know them Injun's can't handle their liquor." Daryl then let out a drunken cackle.

Jimbo ignored his partner and tipped the bottle for Hunter several more times and then he walked back to the fire. Hunter slid down and used the log for a head rest. He pulled a smoke and a match from his top pocket and lit up. He then placed his hat over his face leaving a small crack where he could watch the two men as they prepared to bed down for the night. Hunter had watched the men for several nights studying their sleeping habits in this same fashion.

Daryl was snoring up a storm as the time passed. Jimbo was a light sleeper, and he would have to be taken out first. Hunter slid his hat off and set it on the log behind him. He then sat up and pulled his right knee to his chest and cut the leather strap that bound him with the blade on his boot. He froze for a moment and just stared at Jimbo; the man was still and breathing evenly. Silent like a cat, Hunter stood and walked the three and a half paces to the fire. He never once glanced at Daryl for the sound of his constant snoring told Hunter all he needed to know. Towering over Jimbo, Hunter dropped down putting both of his knees on the sleeping man's chest while at the same time covering his mouth and nose. With the speed of a rattlesnake strike Hunter punched the man in the throat three times very quickly. The first blow broke the man's Adams apple, the second crushed it and the third was for good measure. Jimbo eyes were wide open and he was thrashing around and trying to break free from Hunters weight and choking at the same time. The man was bound tight in a blanket which limited the movement of his legs and feet, but he sure as hell was trying. Hunters hand was over the man's mouth which turned the screams into moans for about ten seconds until Jimbo suffocated and then became still and quiet.

Hunter listened carefully for Daryl's loud drunken snores. The man was sawing logs and drowned the sounds of the night crickets with every long breath.

Hunter closed Jimbo's eyes and walked over to Daryl. He bent over the man and grabbed him by the shirt at the neck. Daryl's eyes opened with a confused look that soon turned to clarity and then surprise followed by fear; right before Hunter punched him in the face hard and knocking him out cold.

Daryl heard his own moaning as he awoke slowly. His head and face hurt and he tasted blood but he weren't sure what had happened. He was on his back and he could feel that his hands and feet were tied at his front. Daryl blinked several times and when his sight came into focus so did the Half-Breed Gunslinger towering over him. He was decked out; The 44's hung from his waist with the Bowie knife tucked into his front belt. Daryl thought; *He's wearin' that knife in the front on purpose so I can see it, son-of-a-bitch!*

Hunter pulled the knife and bent down. Daryl could now see the butt of the shortened shot gun sticking out of his open jacket. Before Daryl could plead for his life Hunter swiped the blade across his throat; the cut was at a precise depth so the man would bleed out slow, but bleed out just the same. As Daryl gurgled, Hunter pulled his pistol and shot it up in the air sending the man's horse running. Dragging Daryl by a rope tied to his feet and off into the night.

Hunter Mounted Zeke and gazed down at Jimbo. He had respected this man for he was just doing his work; but the cowboy had to die for when a man like him was paid to do a job he always followed through. Hunter decided there and then that Captain William B. Hooker was a just man and would keep his word. With Helen and James safe he must ride on and confront those that sought him for their fortune. He would head north and Zig-Zag through the state and search out the bounty hunters that were hunting him. He figured to head off those who would kill him and lead them away from Myakka city, making his friends and family safer for it.

CHAPTER FOUR

Helen awakened with a feeling of alarm, she turned her head to see little James sleeping by her side. She calmed a bit as she looked around the room and allowing her memory to explain her surroundings, it concerned her that Hunter was not there. Her clothes lay on the chair but her guns were gone. She went on instant alert and left the warmth of her bed to dress. The night gown she wore was a loner; she pulled the straps over her shoulders and allowed it to fall to the floor. She slid into her under garments and pantaloons followed by her riding skirt which was wide legged, split and made of suede. She put on her button shirt and then slid her boots over her wool socks. Helen pondered; Hunter would not have left her without her guns; she knew something was not right. While little James slept she left the room and closed the door behind her. As she walked the hall she heard voices up ahead, they were men discussing cattle fencing and payroll. Helen turned the corner and stepped through the doorway and into the smoke filled kitchen. Captain Hooker and two men were sitting at the table drinking coffee in front of their empty food plates. There was a bottle of whiskey in the center of the table and just beyond that was her gun belt hanging on the back of an empty chair.

"Ma'am, feeling right as rain I suspect?" Hooker asked. Helen said nothing. "Take a seat, there's coffee and I'm sure we can rustle up a steak."

Helen headed for the chair on the other side of the table that held her guns, but before she could take another step the Captain blocked her by sliding another chair with his boot.

"This chair will do ma'am, have a seat."

Helen looked into the eyes of the Captain for a moment and wondered why he would not allow her near her gun belt; she sat in the chair provided.

"Where is Hunter James Dolin?"

"Jacks, fetch the lady some coffee." Ordered Hooker, "We have some things to discuss Helen, may I call you Helen?"

She nodded in agreement as the drover set her coffee tin in front of her; he then sat in the chair that held her baby Dragoons.

"Now I know you have questions, and I will explain, but I need you to remain calm, can you do that for me?"

Helen nodded again, as another alarm went off in her head and she was desperately trying to figure out a way to get to her weapons. All three men were armed, the man called Jacks pulled his pistol and set it on top of the table to make the Captains point. The other man in the room that she had not seen before went to stand in the door way.

"Hunter James Dolin is wanted by the law."

"Not by the law," Helen spoke with conviction, "by a mad woman, with a vengeful disposition."

"I have heard of the Montgomery, Dolin feud, It has become quite famous in these parts. I have also heard that the Montgomery clan is all dead or missing? As an ex-lawman it is my duty to allow our court system to make the judgment."

"Judgment?" questioned Helen, "Hunter is a half-breed; the Montgomery's were rich, white and powerful not to mention evil. What kind of judgment do you suppose he will receive?"

"Were rich and powerful? Meaning you have knowledge of their ware-a-bouts?" questioned the Captain. There was a slight pause as Helen and the man stared at one another. "Your concerns are valid ma'am, but it is the process. My men will take you and your boy where ever you wish to go. This ain't no hotel and I have a ranch to run."

"I thank you Captain for your kind hospitality, we will leave at once but I will not have an escort just my horse and gear."

"As is your wish ma'am."

Helen stood and walked around the table for her guns. The man Jacks did not move from the chair that held her weapons.

"Your guns will be returned to you on your way out and not before." said the Captain.

Helen turned and headed for the doorway; the cowboy there stepped aside. She turned to the Captain,

"Where have your men taken Hunter?"

"Fort Foster, one day out now, both men have their orders by me that he will arrive unharmed."

Helen could not hold back a small grin.

"By both men you mean two men, escorting Hunter James Dolin riding his own horse through the swamp?"

Captain Hooker realized what she was getting at, and he suddenly had the feeling he had made a grave mistake. He had an urge to slap that grin right off her face; but instead he took a long draw off the whiskey bottle and hoped she moved on quickly before he forgot he was a gentleman.

"If you can have my horse readied Captain we will leave at once."

Hooker looked to Jacks. The man stood and placed her gun belt over his shoulder and exited the kitchen through another door. Helen quickly went down the hall to grab her son before the gentleman Captain changed his mind.

The man called Jacks was finishing up saddling Helen's horse when she and little James entered the barn. She held the child in one arm and went through the saddle bag; she dug out the harness to carry the child on her back. Little James weren't so little any longer. It was like he grew overnight? He would not fit in the thing no matter how she tried as he began to struggle with her. She set him down and he immediately stopped fussing and just stood there and stared at her.

"You are growin' up like a weed my boy, how old are you anyways?" she asked.

"Momma"

Helen did the figuring in her head and came up with fifteen months maybe. Jacks were standing there watching holding the reins with her guns still hanging over his shoulder.

"Well little James, you held on to Mocha's reins just fine, let's see how you do with Lady?"

Helen took some leather strapping from her saddle bag and tied it around the saddle horn making a short set of reins for James to hold on to. Jacks had a look of doubt on his face and did not answer her request at first, so she repeated it.

"My guns please sir?"

He handed her the belt. She strapped it on and went through a check of the Dragoons. They were empty; she gave Jacks a look.

"The bullets are in the saddle bag, they need to stay there until you're clear of the homestead, Captains orders."

"When I mount will you lift up the boy?"

He nodded and walked over to the child. Helen mounted and Jacks picked the boy up from his under pits and set him in the saddle in the front of his mother. Little James grabbed the reins without being told and was locked in between his mother's lap and the slope of the saddle horn.

"Doggie" said the boy.

"That's right little James, home is where were headed, that's where Mocha waits."

Helen turned Lady and guided her out of the barn ducking through the doorway and headed north. When she passed by the front porch of the ranch home she looked upon Captain Hooker who stood there looking back. They did not speak, but before Helen spurred the mayor into a run she spotted something mounted on the front of the house over the doorway. It was Hunters tomahawk, the one given to him by the Miccosukee Chief, Apayaka Hadjo.

CHAPTER FIVE

Mocha was headed south, a half-day away from Myakka City and following her nose. It was cool out and the air was dry with little or no rain, the spring conditions were perfect for a lasting scent trail. Zeke's and ladies smells were not constant but by following the path Mocha could pick up the horses odors from time to time and keeping her in the right direction. Where ever Hunter and Helen stopped to camp or water, and dismount, their cent would be left behind for the dog's extraordinary sense of smell, 100,000 times as acute as a man's. Mocha also relied on her experience as a swamp dog, born and raised in the wild. Walt always said that dog knows these swamps like the back of her paw.

◆❖◆

Bodie and Bird were packed with goods and heading south tracking Mocha. She had a head start and she was moving fast, not giving the men any rest what so ever. They soon found out that the chocolate Labrador was traveling day and night only resting occasionally. They ran across a kill that looked to be hers. The feathers and carcass of a Black Breasted Red lay in the soil and was covered with fire Ants. Chicken was Mochas favorite meal and her paw prints were easy to spot in the dry, sandy dirt.

Mocha's relentless pursuit seemed somewhat desperate; Bodie and Birds concern grew as they followed. The further they traveled the more they realized that the dog somehow sensed trouble. Hunter, Helen and little James must be in distress, and why not, trouble had followed the gunslinger his whole life.

♦ ❖ ♦

Hunter was heading north, northeast searching for towns and small cities that were scattered throughout this part of the state. He would turn the tables on the bounty hunters by stalking the stalkers. He was the predator now and anyone holding a wanted poster was the prey. Until every paper with his name and likeness was destroyed he would ride, seek and put down his enemies.

The gunslingers plan was to travel east and then west but always moving north, bypassing Myakka City. He would travel clear to the Florida, Georgia line if need be to eliminate his foes. He would then sweep back and end his ride in Myakka City, saving his last stand at his home. The plan would take months into the summer but he was tired of waiting around and looking over his shoulder.

♦ ❖ ♦

Helen and little James were heading north and straight for Myakka city and looking for any signs of Hunter and the men that guided him against his will. Helen was not much of a tracker and only knew what she had learned from watching Hunter, Jebidiah and Walt. She thought she was on the right trail but mostly she would head for Myakka City. Helen knew that Hunter would kill the two cattlemen and escape, this she had no doubt.

Helen would follow their trail for a while and then lose it. She would find it again and then it was gone. She continued on in the direction of Myakka which was in the same general direction as Fort Foster. Helen came upon a fork in the road that forced her to make a decision. One road went to Myakka City and the other veered off to Fort Foster. She stopped Lady and looked down each path. Helen wanted to follow Hunter badly but her first responsibility was to her young son. The gunslinger could take care of him-self, so she took the road that led to home. Little James would be safe with family. Alameda and the Seminole Indian village was also an option she considered. Helen thought she could trust Alameda but not the other Seminoles. She and Hunter had killed Little owl and many of his braves. Little Owl and his men had families and there was no telling how they might react toward her. Home was the safest option so with no more thought she guided Lady toward Myakka City and picking up speed as the day grew late.

The James family was spread out across south Florida searching for one another. Jebidiah and Walt were seasoned soldiers with true grit but getting up in years. They would stay put for now and wait to see if anyone returned to Myakka. Bodie and Bird were younger and stronger, experienced gunmen and full of sass. They were searching to the south for the dog that was searching for Helen and the boy and the gunslinger. Helen was well skilled and pistol trained by Hunter who had yet to meet his equal. She was headed north for the homestead. Apart, each James Family member was someone to reckon with; so far together they were unbeatable.

Hunter's plans were to lead all threats away from his friends. He had saved their lives many times but they would not have been in such positions if it were not for him. He knew this time alone would be short for the loyalty of his friends would soon put them back in danger. When they figured out what he was doing they would search him out to fight by his side, and that was what Hunter did not want. If this were the Half-breed Gunslingers last ride then so-be-it. He wished to do it on his own.

CHAPTER SIX

Hunter rode north/west for some time searching for cities, towns and counties, anyplace there was a sign of a population with a saloon. Information was traded like goods and services for a price and liquor loosened lips.

He was crossing Manatee's Big Prairie, located between Big Cypress and Myakka City when he came across a small town called Punta Gorda, located on the banks of the Charlotte Harbor.

It was mid-day and cloudy and people moved along the dusty street. Rain was beginning to build with the heating of the day across the waterfront. Soon the dust would turn to mud and the wood would be laid in the streets for walking. The horse troughs would be full and the lakes would rise. The wet months were coming with the summer and to the liking of some, farmers mostly.

Hunter dismounted and tied Zeke to the hitching post in front of the saloon. The building was a crude wood structure with bat wing doors. The sounds of poker chips clanking could be heard just outside as he approached; Hunter longed for a simpler time when gambling was his business.

He entered and walked up to the bar. The jangling of his spurs and the thuds of his boots were loud on the wood planked floor, turning heads from the card tables. He stared down the gawker's one at a time until they looked away; out of the nine card players three of them where men to contend with, the others most likely not. Hunter slid a silver coin across the bar and ordered a beer and a bottle. Two men quickly left the saloon sensing trouble. By this time most everyone in these parts knew the half-breed gunslinger. He was a hero to some, a savage killer to others, but to the ones he sought Hunter was nothing more than a payday.

The Bar-keep poured a mug of beer for a man further down the bar, the only man in the room that did not turn toward Hunter at any time. Hunter noticed the tied down guns and decided that he would be the fourth man in the room who might be caring a wanted poster. This man at the bar had somehow gone unseen by Hunter at his first glance of the room; he would be the most dangerous.

The bar- keep made his way in front of Hunter and stood there looking concerned, when he spoke he did so quietly, he was polite but stern.

"Mister, most in here know who you are, the stories are well known and most in these parts back yah." The bar- keep leaned in closer, "there are some in here now..." he paused and glanced side to side, "Yanks that seek your head for re-ward."

Hunter gave the bar-keep a nod to show he understood the warning. He sipped his beer and then sipped his whiskey. He hoped they would give him some time to finish his drinks in peace, but he could already feel the tension building in the smoky still air. Hunter suddenly heard chairs slide across the floor, followed by movement at his right side. He used the mirror that hung on the wall behind the bar to see them coming. He was leaning on the counter top with his hat down as he sipped his whiskey holding the glass in his right hand. Slowly Hunter slid his left hand down and pulled his revolver from the holster; with his thumb on the hammer he waited for the boot sounds on the wood floor as the men moved in toward him. The thuds and clinks of heels and spurs covered the cocking sound as

Hunter pulled the hammer back. He watched the three men position themselves in the reflection of the glass. Two of the men stopped ten feet at his right flank one slightly behind the other as they swept their coats aside to rest their hands on the butts of their pistols. The third man moved in behind Hunter keeping a ten foot distance. Hunter slowly traded the empty shot glass for the beer mug and brought it up for a sip, acting as if he had not noticed the three men that had approached him.

"This is a white man's saloon half-breed," spouted the man to his right, "selling white man's liquor, but since this is your last days you go ahead and finish up that drink."

Hunter was in the middle of a sip when he suddenly slung his half-full beer mug backhanded at the one talking at his right flank while he spun a one eighty to his left facing the man at his back and fired. The shot hit the man center mast before he could draw. The talker closest on his left now, had pulled his revolver, and leveled it as he cocked the hammer; Hunter pivoted further left and cocked the hammer and fired while simultaneously pulling his right revolver. His second shot went through the talkers gut. The third man behind him was trying to get around the gut shot talker as he was flailing backward, his pistol barrel leading the way. The man fired and missed wide while Hunter did not; his third shot from the right handed pistol hit his chest. Hunter continued with the left and then right and emptying both revolvers into each man until they hit the ground dead. Hunter sensed someone directly behind him and close; he dropped his empty revolvers and spun and caught another man by the wrist avoiding getting shot in the back. The man must have come in from the street but he made the mistake of coming to close before firing. Pushing the gun away it went off and the bullet missed his midsection by an inch. With his right hand Hunter had slid the Bowie knife from the small of his back and thrust it upward through the bottom jaw of the intruder. Nothing but gurgles of air through the flow of blood was heard as the life left the bounty hunters eyes. Hunter pulled his knife out and let the body hit the floor with a thud. The knife was covered in the man's blood that ran down to Hunters hand and onto his sleeve. He slung the warm liquid from the knife with several slings of his arm, spots and streams splattered the floor.

The saloon was mostly empty as the remaining patrons had slipped out along with the bar-keep. The only ones left were the three shot and the interloper bleeding from the neck. Hunter was feeling lucky and confused as he spotted the quiet man at the far end of the bar. He had not moved or even looked in the direction of the gunslinger throughout the whole ordeal.

"You gonna' pull them pistols?" Hunter pulled the double barrel out from under his coat and leveled it at the man at the bar. He put his thumb on one hammer but did not pull back just yet.

"You gonna' pull them pistols?" Hunter asked once again.

The man turned his head and looked upon the gunslinger for the first time. There was calm in the older man's eyes that Hunter recognized. This man had killed many and did not fear death.

"No I think not." The man's voice reminded one of a gravel road. His bearded face showed many scars where the hair refused to grow.

"If I see a man holdin' a wanted poster I kill the man holdin' it." Hunter said with conviction.

The veteran at the bar slammed back his whiskey and put his hands up in front of his chest. He then slowly reached in his inside coat pocket and pulled out a folded paper, he then slid it on the bar as far as his arm would allow.

"If I were to draw right here and now, neither one of us would leave this place untouched, almost certain death for the both of us. I did not reach fifty plus years by bein' reckless. Good day sir."

The man tipped his hat, grabbed his bottle from the bar and walked out the front door without looking back. Hunter retrieved his revolvers from the saloon floor and watched the entrance as he reloaded. He walked over to the entry and peeked over the bat wings and into the street; it was deserted and quiet. Hunter moved his way back and went through the pockets of the dead men. He gathered up the wanted posters and lit each one with a match, placing them in a pile on the bar to burn.

Five wanted posters collected, four men dead, the odds were so far in his favor. How many wanted posters did Jane Montgomery print, and how many men would come to collect?

CHAPTER SEVEN

It was early morning and Helen and little James were up on their mount and following the trail north toward Myakka. They were a day and a half ride from town and Helen could hardly wait. It was tough traveling with a toddler by herself even though James was a good boy and had the demeanor of his father. He was quiet and not too fussy, but there were times when he acted his age. Helen was worried about running into trouble with a child in her lap, it would be hard to fight and protect the boy. She was always looking far ahead and searching the landscape for a place to retreat off the path. Lady was a well bred horse and battle tested, she would alert Helen of movement just before the danger arrived. She had other concerns; there was a storm approaching from the west and it looked to be massive coming off the gulf. Helen must reach Myakka City before the storm; there was no other place that she knew, between here and there that held good shelter.

They were moving right along and making good time when suddenly lady's ears went straight up. Helen veered off the path and headed for a patch of pines. The sound of horses could be heard coming up the trail. She did not have time to maneuver through the trees and hide so she made the decision to fight. Little James would have to come along for the ride.

The two horses went by at a fast walk; Helen with her reins in her teeth and both pistols cocked she darted out from behind them moving Lady with small pokes of her spurs.

If not for the turn on the path and a cry from little James, Bird would have lost more than the lobe of his ear. Helen did not miss with her shot but when Bird heard the cry of the child; he pulled on the reins and turned as the bullet nicked his ear. When he yelled out, a fright ran up Helen's spine as she recognized the squawking voice that could only have come from Birdy Boy. Bodie had heard the gun shot and then bird yell out. He turned his horse and with a pistol pulled came back to them. When he saw Helen and the boy he calmed; and then he saw the blood running down Bird's neck.

"You all right Bird?" Bodie yelled.

"What the hell! You shot my ear off!" Bird's horse did a few spins as he fought to get control. Helen rode up beside him and pulled a cotton diaper from the saddle bag, and placed it on his ear applying pressure.

"Is that a clean cotton, shit face is not a nickname I would look forward to?"

"Oh stop fidgeting you big baby."

Little James was giggling at Bird, which made him laugh at himself and Helen was laughing now at the baby and the whole situation. Bodie was not a babbler but he could not help a big smile as he lit a cigarillo.

"Helen where's the gunslinger?" Bodie asked.

"Nice to see you to, Bodie."

"I'm thrilled to death to see you and the boy Ma'am, you must-a missed the smile." Bodie rode in closer as he spoke.

"I know you are glad to see me Bodie." She said with a quick smile before becoming serious. "Hunter was taken by the men of Captain Hooker to Fort Foster for trial."

"I know this Captain Hooker he is a respectable man, too respectable in this case, how many men?"

"Two men for the escort and he was riding Zeke."

"Two men and he were riding Zeke, well?" Bodie said with a slight grin.

"Two men against the gunslinger," said Bird as he was dabbing at his ear with the cotton, "they sure don't know who their dealin' with do they?"

"What are you two doin' out here anyhow?" Helen asked.

Bird answered her with a low voice, "Mocha was just gone one mornin', and she took out after yah."

"We lost her trail a ways back," continued Bodie, "we been guessin' at this point."

A far off rumbling of thunder caught everyone's attention.

"We need to git you back to town ma'am," said Bodie, "a storm is comin' and it looks to be a biggin."

"What about Mocha Bode, she was in my charge?"

"Bird, she's family but she is still just a dog, besides she were born and raised in the wild, she'll be fine."

"He's right Bird," agreed Helen, "I need to git little James to shelter."

"Doggie," said little James.

They turned and headed back to Myakka and keeping ahead of the storm. It looked to cover the entire sky and the clouds seemed to be slowly spinning counter clock wise. Bodie was the only one of the three that was old enough to have seen a storm like this before. He knew what was coming but for now he kept it to himself. Bodie knew that Jebidiah and Walt would see it coming as well and would be taking action to batten down the hatches.

CHAPTER EIGHT

The cracker cowboys had moved on from Myakka early because of the buildup to the west. They headed for their ranches and farms across the state. They were all running from the storm. All business of ranching, farming, rustling, and thievery, whatever one did was put on hold. The Indian war parties would not ride, for the enemy was not the white man now but Mother Nature. Every day normal life would cease until the storm passed and the cleanup was done. There would be structures to rebuild, crops to replant and bodies to bury. The young, the old and the unprepared would be hit the hardest.

Jebidiah and Walt were busy directing the boarding up of windows and doors. Hired locals seeking work and shelter were busy moving animals to the barn and stacking corn, flour and other goods in the third floor rooms of the empty hotel.

A day ago the black and white, once slave named Darnell had wondered into Myakka looking for work. Walt knew the history of the man, but hired him anyway. He had Darnell moving the copper pieces of the whiskey still from the ground floor to the second floor of the saloon. Walt was carefully tearing down the contraption when Jebidiah walked in the saloon to see Darnell moving a copper barrel up the stairs. He waited for the tall man to turn the corner at the top of the second floor before he spoke.

"Is that who I think it is?" Jebidiah asked.

"Yep, that be who you think it is." Walt answered.

"He's a wanted man; don't we have enough of that around here?"

"What's that Jeb, you mean wanted half-breeds? I figure we need the help right now and no bounty hunter will be out lookin'in this storm."

"No, might be seekin' shelter? He's a dangerous man Walt, don't you forget it."

Walt walked behind the bar and poured them both a drink.

"I know'ed of that kid since he was a young boy and his father the slave rapist was also his master and whooped him daily, I figure that man had it comin' when that boy killed him. He's on the run and got nothin' I figure he deserves a chance."

"I ain't arguin' that," replied Jebidiah, "I'm just sayin' be careful for that man is carrin' a big chip on his shoulder."

"He wants meals, drink and a gun by the end of the storm or the week whichever comes first. Then he'll move on." Walt slammed back his shot and poured them both another. "If his work is hard, then that's what I'll do."

"Okay Walt, "replied Jebidiah, "but if that negro boy so much as looks at me wrong ways I'll blow him straight to that plantation in the sky."

"I hear yah Jeb and I'm with yah. I think this one deserves a chance, we've had some pertty good luck with half-breeds in the past don't you think?"

"Mm mm" was all Jebidiah could say as Darnell came back down the stairs; he was a tall man, young and strong. All three men stared at one another and they all knew that he had at least heard the tail end of Walt and Jebidiah's conversation. Walt poured a shot glass and slid it down the bar where Darnell caught it just before it slid off the edge. He nodded a thank you and drank it down; he slid it back empty and then went back to work after giving Jebidiah a look of misgiving.

The City of Miami would receive word on the size and strength of the storm from Naval and shipping fleets by the colored flares shot into the sky. By the time the news hit the swamps of central Florida the storm would be upon them. Whether this was just a tropical storm or a hurricane would depend on the severity of the winds.

The Seminole Indians were already two days on the move for they followed the natural signs provided by Mother Nature. The feeding activity of the animals was more extreme before a storm, for there would be no hunting for food in the bad weather. Extremely calm weather always comes before a storm and the wildlife could sense it approaching days before it could be seen by the human eye. At some point movement to higher ground was the priority. The Indians traveled with the migrating animals and tracking them as far as they would go, the wildlife seemed to know when their distance was safe from the worst of the storm.

Hunter was moving north to the middle of the state and seeking the higher ground. The swamp waters would rise or even flood; the deep woods were the safest place, where the pine trees and great oaks grow. He had made it to Sebring and he planned to head toward the Kissimmee and St Cloud area. The animal movement told him this storm was big so he would ride it out prepare here in Sebring. His pursuit of the bounty hunters would have to wait until the weather passed. He had little time to seek shelter for the storm was coming fast. The closest caves were way up in the panhandle and there were no towns or ranches in this area that he knew of, so his only option was to find a rock formation and build a lean-to. The winds would be strong and he needed a solid wall that would face the coming storm.

Another hour of moving Zeke to the north, the terrain became more and more favorable. Lime rock formations began to break through the ground higher and higher but so far he had not found one high enough to cover the top of the Appaloosa's head. He cursed the flat lands that was Florida and continued on as the purple sky followed. Hunter stopped and observed the storm as it was close enough now to see the movement of the clouds, they were different than a normal thunder storm, there was a counter clockwise spin to them. He figured he had five hours until the rains began and only three hours of daylight. Desperate now he moved the horse faster and hoped the rocky ground would continue. He was looking for a thinning in the trees and then a clearing. The trees would grow sparsely around the lime rock searching for top soil. Finally he found close to what he was looking for; it was not ideal but he was running out of time and the slope was facing the right direction.

Hunter had all his gear except for the tomahawk; it must have been left at Hookers ranch. It was the one thing he needed most right now to cut trees for the lean-to. The bowie knife would work for the smaller branches but for the base of the pines it was far from ideal. Hunter checked his supply of shotgun shells; he would have enough with some left over. He tied Zeke tight just in case he spooked as he then walked to the wooded area. Choosing smaller pines than he would have liked he slid the double barrel shot gun from its holster and pulled the hammers back. Pointing At the base of the pines he pulled the triggers; the loud bang echoed through the woods as the tree fell. He reloaded and blasted another, and then again and again until he had enough downed logs. He used the Bowie to finish off some of the trees that were still attached to their base, and with the knife he stripped the smaller green branches and laid them in a pile.

Time was against him; he hoped the lean-to would be just good enough for shelter, depending on how bad was the storm. He dug three holes with the Bowie, one foot down opposite of the rock ledge and planted three of the thickest logs, straight up into the hole. He had gathered some vines and pulled some twine from the saddle bag. Holding up one log horizontal against the planted ones he tied them together with the twine. He then tied another log at the bottom and then one in the middle. The wood wall was lower than the rock wall done on purpose. Hunter then laid shorter logs from the top of the rock wall to the top of the wood wall tight together to form the roof. Using twine he tied tight each roof poles to the top of the wood wall poles. He took his bear skin from his gear and went to the top of the ledge and placed it long ways over the top of the logs that rested there. He then laid the last three tree poles on top, long ways and tied off the ends with the remaining twine and some vines he had cut earlier. The wind began to pick up and the sky was turning dark as he collected loose rocks and boulders for weight on top of the tied poles that lay over the bear skin. The water would roll off the bear skin in the middle of the lean-to, helping to keep him and Zeke somewhat dry in the middle of their shelter.

Satisfied that there was enough weight to hold down the top, Hunter went to the pile of small branches stripped from the pines earlier and laid half of what he had on top of the slanted roof, spread out but side by side covering the bear skin. With the bowie knife in hand Hunter drudged up the hill till he reached an area where some five foot cabbage palms grew. He used the big knife like a machete and chopped many palm fronds from the trees. He made many trips laying them flat on top of the roof and laying heavy branches on top of the fronds to keep the wind from blowing them off. Four trips it took to cover the lean-to's roof with the palm fronds and tree branches, by this time the wind was blowing harder and the rain began to fall, light but steady.

Hunter had to stop the building for a time and collect downed branches from around the woods for a fire before the rain soaked them. This took precious time but it must be done. He stacked the fire wood under the roof in a pile, enough for two fires; hopefully the storm would pass through quickly.

The last thing to do was to take the long strings of vines and rap them under and over the roof to tie it all together. Hunter felt he needed more vine, but before he left to cut more he led Zeke into the shelter and out of the rain. The horse was glad to go inside for he had been in such structures several times before in bad weather. The twelve foot high, by eight foot wide, by twelve foot long lean-to suddenly got much smaller when the horse was brought inside, but it would have to do.

Hunter returned with long vines dragging behind him and then he wrapped and tied them around the roof until they were used up. That was all he could do for time was up as the wind blew, the rain was now stronger and thunder began to rumble. He removed Zeke's saddle which would be his dry seat, and brushed the horse down. He left the reins on the Appaloosa for if the thunder and lightning were tremendous he might need to aid comfort and keep him calm. The horse did not spook easily but if the storm was too bad and the shelter did not hold they could be in a world of hurt.

The storm came quickly which was a good sign for it was moving fast, meaning it could be over just as quick. Zeke was watered earlier in the day while passing a creek on their way to the higher ground, at that time Hunter allowed the horse to graze for a time. Natural grasses were good but did not have the nutrients that hay, or grains like corn, oats and barley stored. Zeke was used to 5 pounds of mostly corn a day which was minimal for a horse and the supplies were very low. Sugar cubes helped and Hunter always stocked up on wild apples when possible.

Hunter ate Jerky and drank coffee over a small fire set at the rear side of his horse at one end of the lean-to. So far the water was running off the short end of the roof as designed and they were dry under it. The wind blew around them as the position of the rock wall was set dead-on. If the wind continued blowing in this same direction they would weather the storm without incident. As Hunter thought this the wind grew stronger and began to swirl and the rain came down harder. The roof began to drip here and there but most of the water rushed down the sides of the roof like a water fall on all three sides. Hunter used his hat to catch the water and held it for Zeke to drink his fill after empting his feed bag. The thunder and lightning were spread out and manageable for Zeke. Florida was known for its thunder storms and the appaloosa had grown familiar.

With nothing left to do but wait, Hunter lit a cigar and sat on the saddle, leaning against the rock wall, he began to nod off; his last thoughts were that of his woman and child before sleep overcame him.

◆❖◆

The storm lasted two days; after the first day it began to slow as the eye passed and then it hammered them and their shelter for another day, before moving on to the east and breaking up slowly. Hunter figured another day and the storm would clear completely. The remaining rain on the back end of the storm was steady and the wind continued but slowed as each hour passed. As the storm calmed the gunslinger began to get a feel for his surroundings once again and the feel was that he was not alone. He sensed another close by as he looked and listened through the open end of the structure. Friend or foe was what he could only question.

Hunter dressed fully and ducked out of the lean-to. He looked and listened for any sign through the light wind and rain; there was nothing and then he caught a whiff of smoke from a fire that was not his.

Hunter went back inside the shelter and saddled Zeke and prepared him for a quick getaway. He strapped the feed bag on with a half ration of corn and then watered him from his hat. It took patients to fill his hat for the rain was running slow off the roof. It took almost an hour to fill the Stetson five times until Zeke was full.

Hunter checked all his weapons before he stepped back out into the light but steady flow of rain. He back tracked his way to where he had entered the clearing; if he were being followed they would be behind him or at his flanks. Hunter crept low and looked to the sky for the signs of smoke. Through the trees he saw a tendril of smoke that died quickly from the wind and rain but it was there. Slow anger was building in him. He did not like to be hunted. If the man was a foe, he planned to collect the bounty on Hunter dead or alive.

Hunter came around a ledge of rock and there it was; forty yards away there stood a lean-to where the smoke had come from. It was set up like his but more crudely built. The branches that held the roof were thin and dead. Not cut but collected down fall. Hunter drew his gun and judged the distance; he fired his revolver. He pulled the hammer back with is thumb and fired again.

Cut by the bullets, the corner of the structure fell and the roof folded toward the rock and spooking the horse. A black came out kicking and bucking through the brush and ran off away from him and into the woods. He watched the smoke thicken as it smoldered around the downed structure.

Hunter thrust his gun back into his holster and pulled the other. He wanted six shots going in. He saw slight movement behind the collapsed branches but no one appeared.

Hunter moved quickly to another hiding place behind a downed pine tree. He was only twenty yards away now from the man's hideout. Hunter decided he would not be followed when he left this place. He would not leave here until it was settled.

"Come out." Hunter yelled, even knowing he would reveal his position.

"Come out with hands empty or come out shootin'."

There was only silence... and then the man came with an attack from around the far side of the shelter with rifle in hand. The man knew where to aim his fire from the sound of Hunter's voice: he managed two shots high, but by the time he zeroed in on his exact position the gunslinger had fired and caught him in the chest. The rifle dropped and the man fell against the downed roof and rolled to the ground, coming to rest on his back.

Hunter walked nearer with the Colt cocked and ready. He looked down at the lean man, who was bearded and had a scar that ran down his left cheek. Their eyes met. Blood soaked the man's clothes; the shot was a fatal one.

"Where's the poster?"

"Coat," The man said with a bloody cough, "inside pocket."

Hunter pointed the revolver barrel at the man's head and with his empty hand he dug through the blue coat until he found the wanted poster.

"I hope you die... and die hard." The man gasped with a weak but angry voice.

"You first Mr. Yankee-doodle." Said Hunter as he drew down and fired.

The man's heart exploded and his eyes closed for the last time.

Hunter walked to the far side of the wrecked lean-to and placed the rolled wanted poster in the smoldering coals of the fire, he then lit his smoke with the paper. He left it to burn and then emptied the dead man's pockets before heading back to fetch Zeke.

The rain and wind was easing as he tracked down the dead man's black. The horse had not gone far and was found grazing in a small meadow down below. The man's supplies were low but Hunter took what he could use before relieving the horse from his gear and setting him free. He would have liked to have kept the black but it was marked and he could not risk it. The horse was left to roam and Hunter knew he would eventually become the property of the Seminoles as they traveled this part of the territories.

Hunter was headed for Brevard County, a railroad and steam boat town on the edge of what the Indians called the Kissimmee River. A place he had visited once back in the day. It was a rough place with hard men all looking for coin and willing to kill for it. He figured this would be a good place to collect some wanted posters. Hunter would not stop hunting the hunters until all the papers with his name on it were no more.

Chapter Nine

Bodie, Bird, Helen, and little James rode out the storm with Jebidiah and Walt in Myakka City. The hurricane moved through quickly and had lost some steam as it crossed land. The damage was minimal and the blessings against storms that the Seminole Indians had put on the region seemed to work once again.

The James family was incomplete with two missing. The Gunslinger and Mocha were out there somewhere and the family would not rest until they were all back together again. They were in the eating room on the first floor of the hotel sitting around the big table. Bessie was bringing plates of vittles as they discussed what must be done.

"Well I'm goin'," said Helen, "Hunter would not sit still if anyone of us were out there. Bessie will take care of little James while I am gone."

Bessie set a plate down and her eyes met Helen's as she said this, Bessie nodded in agreement with a smile. Helen smiled back and then continued,

"Where is he Jeb, have we heard anything?"

"What we do know is they did not make it to Fort Foster and the men that were his captures did not make it back to the ranch."

Walt chimed in on the conversation.

"My guess is them men are dead and the gunslinger is escaped. If he'd gone back to Hooker's ranch we'd know that by now. Where he done went too I could not say."

"I been thinkin' about that," said Bodie, "thinkin' about what he thinks and then what I might do. Like I'm sayin' this is just a guess…

Bodie paused for a time collecting his thoughts.

"Will you done spit it out!" said Walt with some irritation.

"Alright," said Bodie with his hands up, "If you had wanted posters with your face on um floatin' around out there wouldn't you want to round them up? Cuz as long as they're out there with five thousand dollars on your head, men will keep comein' for ya."

"I'm gonna find him and fight by his side, now whose goin' with me? Helen asked.

I'll be goin with ya," said Bird, "but I'll be goin' also to find Mocha for she was my responsibility."

"Honey," said Helen in a calmed voice, "Mocha will be followin' Hunter's path I reckin', just like us."

Helen gave Bird a reassuring smile for she knew the boy's guilt over the missing dog was working him over.

Jebidiah stood from his meal.

"It's settled then, we're all goin, we got some weeks before them cracker cowboys could even think about movin' herds after this storm. We got good people that can keep the saloon and the stables if we ain't back by then. Lamb runs the post and he is in charge. I think we should close the hotel; there are rooms at the saloon for any stragglers if needed."

Jebidiah looked to all, they all agreed with head shakes around the room, all except Walt; all eyes rested on him.

"I guess it wouldn't matter none if I said I was too old for this shit?" Walt asked, they all shook their heads in disbelief with smiles and laughter, "All right then," Walt continued, "quit eye ballin' me, and let's git a packin'."

The James family spent the day gathering supplies, as much as they could carry for travel. They would hunt and fish along the way as needed. Two pack horses would follow in tow, loaded down with grain for the horses, coffee, sugar, ammunition and whiskey. Water supply for man and horse was not a problem in the swamps especially after the storm. The problem would be high waters and downed trees and other debris. Wild life would be on the move searching for food after three days of lockdown. The over filled swamps would push gators and snakes further inland, bears, bobcats and panthers would be on the hunt; all dangerous in their own ways.

Indians were always a problem but the James family had an advantage; they had Helen, she was known to be the woman of Lustee –Manito- Nakanee. The Seminoles of the Miccosukee Clans revered the gunslinger as a great warrior and they feared killing him for it would release his black heart across the land. They still believed this to be true for after Hunter had killed Little Owl and his renegade warriors the Snake Clan had not come for him. They would have attacked Myakka city within days as was their nature, if they did not believe he had power. Walt and Jebidiah rode with this hope, but they would be on alert for trusting Indians was not at all in their nature.

The hurricane had wiped away all tracks. Mocha had headed south, so that is where they would start their search, not knowing that Hunter was already far too their north.

CHAPTER TEN

Traveling was slow for all across the state were downed trees, high waters, muddy trails and the animals were on the move feeding for the first time in days. Hunter new his way to the steamboat town in Brevard County but landmarks had changed or disappeared altogether after the storm. Men used the stars and sun for direction and their memories to find places they had been before. Landmarks like great trees, rock formations and manmade structures were guides for travel.

Hunter's memory served him well and he found the short road that led to the town. Zeke walked slowly at Hunters direction down the thoroughfare passing buildings and onlookers, his head was held high and he was on the alert. Hunter had cocked the hammers on the shot gun at the edge of town; it lay ready under his buckskin coat. He was headed for the saloon and hoped he would have time for a drink before being noticed. As usual hoping did not make anything so.

Across from the saloon was the sheriff's office where three men with repeating rifles in hand stepped off the porch and into the road. The door was propped open and a large man, cleaned shaven with a chiseled face came forward. He stopped slightly in front of the other men.

"Can I help you sir?"

So much for that drink, Hunter thought, as he steered Zeke to their side of the road. He stopped, facing the men and leaving ten feet in-between them. Hunter said nothing.

"Names Hannigan," the large man pulled his duster back showing his badge and uncovering his revolver, "this is my town and if there's trouble, my men and I will have the last say."

"I'm just passin' through sheriff."

"When you say passin' through, you mean stayin' on your horse and not stoppin'." Hannigan said this as an directive and not a question.

"I planned on gittin' a drink and a meal before movin' on."

"I know who you are Half-breed, and I know there are at the least three men in that saloon holdin' posters with your face on um."

"There's no one left to pay that bounty sheriff." Hunter replied.

"That may be true, but them bounty hunters don't know it and I'm fairly certain they won't take your word on that?"

"I don't know sheriff, I can be pretty convincin'."

"I'm paid to keep the peace in this town gunslinger," said Hannigan, "and that's what I'll do."

When Hannigan said this the three men cocked the levers on their Henry rifles but kept the barrels down. Hunter's eyes narrowed and fanned quickly from one man and then the other. He was prepared to draw.

'Easy gunslinger," said the sheriff, "you're free to go, but go you will."

Hunter stared them down for a quiet moment contemplating his next move. The times were changing; if he killed just one of these lawmen it would bring the U.S. Army down on him quicker than one could say 'Hang em high'

There were men in that saloon hunting him and he would not give them a pass.

"Alright sheriff, I reckin' I'll move on, but I will ask you a favor for my cooperation?"

Hannigan turned his palms up in a wait for his request.

"Let the word out I was run outta town, and then point the direction I was headin' in."

"Alright gunslinger, what you do outside my jurisdiction ain't my concern. Hell, I don't care much for bounty hunters anyhow, in my book they're just paid killers without honor."

Hunter tipped his hat and turned Zeke with a tug of the reins, moving him down the road. When they reached the edge of town he spurred the Appaloosa for a while making sure his tracks were easy to follow in the muddy sand. He knew they would come; for five thousand dollars would make men push pass their limitations.

Hunter did not like it, but Zeke would have to be the bait and left in the open to lure them in. An ambush was not very honorable but he had too much to do with little time and too much ground to cover. An ambush was one of the bounty hunters favorite tools; Hunter could play the same game and he would do so to survive.

Zeke was tied loosely to a tree just off the beaten path. Hunter followed a clearing and entered a patch of forest made up of southern pines, Australian pines and Great Oaks. He climbed fifteen feet up to a chosen branch of one oak that overlooked the clearing. The Henry rifle was slung over his shoulder; it was a sixteen shot .44 caliber rim fire, lever action, breech loader.

Hunter settled in and made himself as comfortable as possible. Not knowing how long he would have to wait, comfort was important. The last thing he wanted was for his muscles to stiffen or worse yet cramp up. After the first few shots he would have to move quickly and face his enemy. He had relieved himself before climbing the oak and he now chewed jerky and chased it with whiskey from a flask. It was a cloudy day which helped conceal his wear-a-bouts in the dense woods. If the sheriff did his part he would not have to wait long. Five thousand dollars would be the one thing that would entice men to leave a comfortable saloon and risk their lives out in the open.

After a smoke, Hunter closed his eyes and drifted off into sleep, but not deeply, his ears were still wide awake and listening for the signal. An hour and a half had passed when he heard Zeke's low nicker; it was very faint but there none the less. This was Zeke's warning of approaching horses or danger. They had perfected this warning signal over the years. Hunter cocked the rifle; resting it in the crook of a branch he aimed it at the only spot where they could approach the clearing.

He did not know how many would come, at the least there would be three, if the sheriff's information was right? Hunter listened intently and watched closely for some time. He wondered if it were a false alarm; and then a stick snapped underfoot. They most likely left their horses and were stalking him. The first man appeared, He waited until all four men were in the clearing and then he fired taking the first one out with a shot to the chest. The others spread to the edge of the woods firing in his direction, but it was clear they had not pinpointed him just yet. Hunter cocked the lever and hit one in the hip grazing him just before he ducked in behind a tree. A wounded man could be more dangerous as he felt his time was short and he had nothing to lose. Hunters bad shot had just created such a state.

Hunter climbed down the back of the tree and using it for cover. He dropped to the ground and moved away some before circling and heading for the wounded man's flank. He left the rifle at the base of the tree as the men were now firing on his old position. It took some time for Hunter to flank them. He must hurry for they would figure out his movements soon.

Hunter snuck in behind the wounded man. He pulled his Bowie knife and in one swift motion he grabbed the man's chin at his back and cut his throat. After dropping him to the forest floor he pulled his Colt and walked out into the clearing. The bounty hunters were still firing up in the tree occasionally and did not see the gunslinger walk out onto the path. Hunter waited until their revolvers clicked dry before he pulled his Colt.

"Billy!" The man yelled out as he reloaded. "Where'd he go at Billy?"

"Here," said Hunter.

The bounty hunters turned and fired; Hunter slammed the hammer three times standing in the middle of the clearing. The closer man named Billy, shot wide and his second shot went straight up as he fell dead. The other man was slow in reloading and never got off a shot before Hunter unloaded into his mid- section. Three bodies lay motionless on the path and one lay silent in the woods. Hunter went through the pockets of the men in the clearing one at a time. On bended knee he opened a folded paper taken from the last man's coat pocket. He was looking upon a poor likeness of himself, when the sound of a hammer clicked behind him and then a voice.

"Hands to heaven friend, don't think I won't splatter your brains all over this ground."

Hunter did not move. He heard another man coming through the brush.

"Shoot him Joe! Paper says dead not alive."

"Shut up Boone, I got the drop on um. Let us see them hands half-breed nice and slow."

Hunter slowly put his hands up and out with the poster still held in his grasp.

"Now stand even slower and turn around."

"Shoot him Joe!"

"Shut up Boone. I'm not draggin' him through these woods if I don't hafta."

Hunter turned slow and stood facing the two men. There were no doubt they were close kin, one older and then the younger. The older had a Springfield rifle pointed at his head at a distance of ten feet. The younger was by his side but two feet further back pointing a single barrel shot gun. Both men carried single revolvers. Hunter knew right away that these men weren't bounty hunters but locals looking to cash in.

"The payers of this bounty are dead, there is no reward." Hunter waved the paper slightly.

"And how might you know that half-breed?" asked the older.

"Cuz I killed them."

"I might say that too if I were in your predicament."

"Just shoot him Joe!"

"Shut up! Boone! Mister, you move real slow and with the free hand drop that pistol belt."

Hunter knew he could draw and kill the rednecks but he would most likely take some buck shot at the least. The younger was so jittery Hunter was troubled he might squeeze that trigger out of sheer panic. The older had the looks of a war veteran and would not miss with the long barrel at this short distance.

Hunter unhooked his belt and dropped his guns. The bowie knife fell with them. Sometimes he tucked the blade in his pants at the small of his back but this time it was only in the belt, *Bad luck,* he thought.

Hunter was thinking his only chance was to draw these two in closer somehow when he heard a rustle in the brush off to his right. Out of nowhere a dark blur lunged at the farthest, younger man holding the shot gun; it went off with a boom to the left. Hunter buckled down and grabbed a pistol from the grounded sheath. At the same time the closer, elder man was turning to see what was happening behind him. That is when Hunter shot the man in the side of the head. He fell forward as Mocha was ripping on the face of the younger; he was screaming.

"Mocha heel! Mocha!"

She backed off the man who was rolling around on the ground and whimpering. Hunter walked over to him and with one shot to the head he put him down from his misery.

Hunter went to one knee and Mocha nearly knocked him down with kisses. She had burs and stickers in her fur and on her legs and belly was wet mud layered on top of dried mud.

"You are a mess girl. You followed me, and then you saved me. I am in your debt always."

Mocha turned her tail to him, so he obliged by scratching her backside. When Hunter scratched her right hip she would turn her head to the right and when he scratched her left hip she would turn her head back to the left.

"Character is something you got plenty of dog." Said Hunter as the brown Labrador had now turned to face him. Mocha shook her head after Hunter gave a good scratching to the ears.

Hunter stood and whistled sharply. Mocha's ears went straight up and then ran to meet Zeke as he appeared in the clearing. Zeke whinnied and shook his head up and down. Mocha did circles around the horse while barking, and then the dog sat and stared at the saddle bag where the jerky was held.

"Nothin' wrong with your memory dog." Hunter said as he pulled beef strips from the pouch and tossed them to her; she scarfed them down with hardly a chew.

Hunter went around to each dead man with Mocha by his side and collected the posters with his name upon them. He raided money, tobacco and ammunition from all. The guns he buried in a discreet, marked location. He made a map on where to find them if he ever was in this area and needed weapons. A man's guns could be identified and used as evidence against him. Hunter had done this before and had guns buried throughout the State. A half-breed gunslinger that had been wanted most of his life would have a hard time convincing anyone that he had killed in self-defense.

Hunter burned the posters in a pile on the forest floor and left the bodies for the turkey buzzards and worms. This was some of the only times that Hunter was slightly glad that Helen was not with him, for she would insist that they bury these men. In Hunter's mind the souls of these men had already been decided, and whether or not the rituals of man were implemented would make no difference.

Hunter mounted Zeke and moved out with Mocha following by his side. He planned to find a watering hole for the warmest part of the day and give Mocha a well needed scrub. Hunter lifted his arm and took a sniff; *the dog ain't the only one that needs a good bath.*

CHAPTER ELEVEN

Walt had led them south for two days on main traveling routes and searching for tracks of the dog. The storm had washed away most signs of any kind. Walt did find a few remaining paw prints but then lost Mocha's tracks for a time as she made her own path through the thicket. On the other side of the half mile of undergrowth Walt found Mocha's paw prints were she had exited. He took the credit for being a great tracker but he knew this time it was pure luck, which he would take any day. The dog had changed direction from the south to the north east for no apparent reason other than she must be following scent with her nose?

Back on the path Jebidiah rode second, with Helen in the cradle of the convoy, then Bird and Bodie took the rear. They were moving quickly now with good tracks to follow and they were now making good time. They were happier on the trail, beating the brush in search of the dog and the Gunslinger. Waiting around and doing nothing was not in their nature.

Another day had passed when they came across the shelter were Hunter had weathered the storm. Mocha's tracks led them directly under a flock of circling turkey buzzards. They stopped at a distance as the smell of death reeked through the woods.

"I got this." Bodie said as he dismounted and tied a bandana over his nose and mouth. He shooed the buzzards away to get a look. Helen found it difficult to breathe as she waited for a response.

Bodie backed away and walked quickly back.

"A white man, his boots are military, Yankee issue."

Helen let out a sigh of relief.

"Well, there's one less bounty hunter to worry about." Jebidiah said.

"Let us git," said Bird, "Before I lose my stomach."

"Let us go then," said Bodie, "We got to pick the tracks back up."

"I got um over here!" yelled Walt. "Come on, foller me."

They were moving faster now for there were two sets of tracks to follow, Zeke's hoof prints as well as Mocha's.

The sun was hanging low in the sky when they came across a small doe drinking from a small stream of rain water. Walt raised a fist and stopped. He pulled his rifle; aimed and fired. The deer sprinted four quick steps and then went down hard with a high neck shot. They rode over to the kill and dismounted.

"Nice shootin' there Walt," Jebidiah said. "Not bad for a blind son-of-a- bitch."

"Eatin' nothin' but jerky for two days can sharpin' a sons-a- bitch's eye."

"Boys," said Helen, "we don't have time for a cook-out."

"I hear ya little lady," answered Jebidiah, "we been goin' hard for days and these horses too, some real food and a little rest is all I ask."

Bodie dismounted and walked over to the kill, "Look, continue on and find us a camp spot for the night, me and Bird will skin this pup and catch up with ya."

"Helen?" asked Jebidiah.

Walt chimed in on the conversation before Helen could answer.

"Darlin', I can't follow them tracks at night without a clear moon anyways, them clouds are still rollin' about and its gittin' late."

After a sigh and a pause, Helen agreed reluctantly. "Til the morn then, but I want to be on the road at first light."

All accepted and then they went on about their duties. Jebidiah, Walt and Helen found a suitable place to camp three quarters of a mile from the kill site. Bodie and Bird made quick work of the deer and caught up with the rest within an hour. Walt had the fire prepared with a spit for cooking and was sitting on a downed log sipping whiskey.

Jebidiah had ridden the perimeter of the camp for anyone that might be a threat. They were alone for a half mile in any direction, but would still post a guard through the night.

They gorged themselves with the grilled venison and sipped whiskey. They smoked cigars and told tales of the half-breed gunslinger. When one story included Mocha, Bird took his rifle and walked off into the night to stand first watch.

"He's taking the dog gone missin' hard." Walt said with some sadness in his voice.

"He has come to love that dog," answered Bodie, "I told him there is no way he could have known Mocha would wander off like that, she showed no sign."

"That dog was born and bred in these swamps," said Jebidiah, "Hell, she might be more prepared to live out here than we is?"

"We will find Mocha and Hunter, and at least they found each other." Helen said, "And no more splittin' up, from now on we stay together."

They slept hard and woke early; they drank coffee in the dark before first light and then moved out with the break of the sun. They figured two days or less until Mocha and the gunslinger were found.

Chapter Twelve

Hunter found a spring fed watering hole and rode Zeke down into the water up to the horse's neck. Mocha followed them in swimming around and barking loudly. The spring suddenly deepened forcing Zeke to swim; the horse turned back around, got his footing and shot out of the cold water and back onto dry land. Hunter dismounted and Mocha came alongside him and shook.

"Hey Dog really, you got to do that right here next to me?"

Hunter built a fire and then stripped Zeke of his gear, setting the leather in the afternoon sun to dry. He stripped his clothes off down to his state of nature, and then hung his wears on tree branches. He brushed down Zeke and strapped on his feed bag.

Hunter shared some jerky with Mocha which she barley chewed before swallowing. With his bare butt on the grounded saddle he used the horse brush on the dog. He scraped caked mud from around her legs and feet and pulled burrs from her fur. Mocha sat still and seemed to enjoy the brush but most of all she waited for treats that Hunter pulled from the saddle bag.

The shot gun lay across his bare lap and his pistol belt hung on the saddle horn by his side. They were in the middle of nowhere, but you never knew who might be out there lurking.

Hunter used the fire to finish the drying of his clothes before he dressed fully. He heard the whistles of the Bob White as the sun dropped. He decided to hunt for the quail first thing in the morning. Taking a covey of quail could feed them for tomorrow and maybe the next day.

They slept by a small fire through the night without incident and woke before the sun.

Mocha turned out to be one hell of a bird dog. She flushed out the quail from under the brush and Hunter used the shot gun aiming for the head so not to blast the breast apart. Digging small led balls from a bird's breast meat was common with a bad shot or to close a range. Within two hours they had seven birds to pop the heads, pluck and roast over the fire. He cooked them all; he ate two and one for Mocha and the rest were packed away for later. Three hours after sun up they were back on the trail searching for the next town to collect wanted posters with his likeness upon them.

◆❖◆

The James Family found the spring fed water hole at noon along with Hunters distinguished fire. Walt and Helen were off their horses and searching the grounds.

"We're right on his ass now." Walt said as he retraced the steps. "They bathed and slept here by a fire."

Walt went toward the brush and walked along the edge. He went down on one knee with a moan. He gathered up a hand full of feathers and examined them for a moment and then stood with an even louder groan.

"He shot a mess of Bob Whites and ate before moving off in that direction." Walt said, as he massaged his knee cap.

"How long Walt?" Helen asked as she followed his steps.

"I'd say, two maybe three hours, and movin' steady."

Helen mounted up and then Walt.

"We will be moving fast," Helen announced, "by the end of this day I want to be eating supper all of us together."

Walt led the way riding as fast as he could and still track their direction. Jebidiah and Walt did not speak it, but they both had an idea where the gunslinger was headed. If they were right, Hunter would for sure need their help.

Chapter Thirteen

In the late afternoon Walt came across some disturbing tracks. He and Jebidiah jumped from their mounts and began to read the story that the ground marks told.

"What is it?" asked Helen.

Jebidiah and Walt walked around, kneeling and scraping the dirt with their gloved hands.

"Walt, Jeb, talk to me." Helen demanded.

Walt stood and spoke up,

"We got un-shod horses, some shod and some missing shoes, about ten maybe twelve."

"Renegade Injuns," Bodie said as he moved his horse up and alongside Helen.

"They surrounded Hunter and the dog right here." Jebidiah said with some concern.

Walt had moved to the north on foot and had been out of everyone's sight for a few minutes before he returned.

"I don't know how or why but the renegades let him pass." Walt said, "Hunter let out quick with Mocha followerin'."

"What about the Injuns?" Bodie asked.

"They're followerin' him slow, I don't git it?"

"Well," said Jebidiah, "then we follow, but we best be on alert and ready for anythin'."

The sounds of clicks and spins of cylinders echoed through the woods as they all checked their weapons and preparing for battle. Jebidiah and Walt mounted up and led the way as they tracked the renegades that where following the gunslinger.

There were twelve Indians that had surrounded Hunter, some from different Miccosukee clans in Florida and a few from a lower Creek tribe in the Carolina's. The ones that had only heard few stories of Lustee-Manito- Nakanee were willing to fight the gunslinger but two of the renegades were from the Snake Clan and they had witnessed the gunslinger in action. The killing of Little owl was no small feat. Hunter was ready to draw and Mocha growled low. Hunter calmed the dog from the start for the Indians would not think twice about placing a bullet or an arrow in the animal. Zeke's ears were pinned back and his eyes were wide.

Hunter was dead on accurate with his guns and up to this point he had been extremely lucky but twelve against one at this distance he would kill three to five at best. Running was not an option, for the area of the path were they had surrounded him was too long a stretch and very narrow, a bullet in the back would be the result.

Hunter's hands were ready to draw but for now he listened to the arguing that ensued. The two Indians from the Snake Clan feared the gunslinger and they explained their concern to the others. Killing the half-breed would release the evil from inside his black heart upon the land and would follow them to their death.

The twelve braves had not yet decided on a leader; one Indian from the north was young, strong and angry and he was clearly looking to establish himself. He steered his horse alongside Hunter, and faced him. Their eyes met in a stare down. After a moment it was clear that there was no fear in either man, but at the end doubt crept into the Indians look; Hunter's steel blue gaze did not waver.

With a few words the renegades parted and allowed Hunter to pass. It was clear that fighting the gunslinger was not worth the reward at this time, a reward meaning honor and glory. If there was someone left to pay the bounty on the Half-breed gunslinger no Whiteman would pay Indians for any bounty.

As soon as Hunter cleared their sight he set Zeke into a gallop, and when he was out of ear shot he spurred the horse into a run with Mocha keeping pace without trouble. It had been Hunters experience that young Seminole warriors could not be trusted to keep their minds made. The young leader would stew over backing down and eventually his pride would force him to confront the gunslinger.

Hunter stopped Zeke slowly at the edge of a wide part of the trail and dismounted. He slid the rifle from the saddles sheath, and then grabbed the telescope from its place. He dug a piece of jerky from the saddle bag and tossed it to the dog. Mocha caught it in mid-air and with two chews and a sucking sound the meat was gone.

"You go with Zeke Mocha, shadow her girl" Hunter tapped the bag with the jerky and smacked the horse lightly on the hind quarters. Zeke took off down the trail and Mocha followed.

Hunter climbed a giant oak set back off the path a good twenty feet up to where he could stand on a branch behind the main trunk. He knew that the Indians were more likely to check the trees than most white men but he hoped this old trick might still work.

He pulled the scope to its full length and began to scan his back trail. In a circular view he spotted the braves searching after him. *That didn't take long.* Hunter thought. Something made him scan further back with the scope; to his shocking surprise he saw Walt and Jebidiah coming into view and tracking the Indians.

"Damn crazy old coots." Hunter murmured.

He then saw Helen, Bird and Bodie come into view just behind Walt and Jebidiah.

That evens up the odds a bit. Hunter thought.

The renegades were in the saddle walking their horses down the path single file and tracking him. The James family was about to run up on the braves. Walt knew they were close; Hunter watched with the scope as Walt raised his bald up fist, he then drew his weapon and the others did the same.

This battle was going down and Hunter would draw first blood. He pocketed the scope and aimed the rifle at the ear of the leading Injun and squeezed the trigger. He was aiming high for the distance was significant. The crack of the rifle alerted everyone as the Indian grabbed his bloody neck and fell from his horse. Hunter cocked the lever and aimed for the fifth red man in line and shot him in the chest as he tried to turn his horse on the narrow path. Two of the braves up front got a bead on where Hunter was firing from and they fired on him; Hunter ducked behind the trunk of the tree as bark splattered in the air inches from his face. The Indians at the rear of the line turned to retreat and surprisingly found themselves face to face with Walt and Jebidiah coming up the trail. Shots were ringing out from all directions now. The Indians at the back were caught off guard and went down hard as Walt and Jebidiah were side by side and empting their weapons. Helen squeezed her horse in-between the old men with both her Dragoons drawn. She took down two Injuns with her fire, so to allow Walt and Jebidiah to reload under her cover. Bird and Bodie had squeezed through tree branches and splitting the old men so they could get to the front and help Helen. The horses were hard to handle in the confined area and they did not like being pushed into the brush at the sides of the trail; but the horses did their jobs like well-trained soldiers.

At the front Hunter killed two more with the rifle which sent the remaining Renegades retreating to the back. They were headed straight for Helen. Hunter climbed down and then jumped the last ten feet from the tree and ran toward the path with his revolvers drawn.

Bird and Bodie got passed Walt and Jebidiah through the smoke filled trail to find Helen grappling with a brave who was trying to pull her off her horse. Neither man had a clear shot and was being fired upon from several Indians behind Helen and up the trail. Bird killed one and then yelled out as he was hit. Bodie fired back killing the remaining two. As the smoke cleared and the shooting stopped; there was Helen on the Indians horse, he had her in a choke hold with a blade held at her temple.

No one dared to move toward Helen and the savage.

"You okay Bird?" Bodie asked without taking his eyes off of Helen and the Injun who held her hostage.

"Yeah Bode, just a nick. Son-of-a-bitch shot me!"

"Are you okay dammit?"

"Yes! It just hurts like hell, went clean through hardly any meat."

Walt and Jebidiah crammed their way to the sides and behind Bodie and Bird. They all had their guns drawn but the Indian had Helen blocking any shots as she was between him and them. There was tension in the air.

"Let the woman go or die." Jebidiah said this with conviction.

The Indians eyes were wide but he showed no sign of surrender.

A short moment went by, which seemed like an eternity. Then the Indian saw a change in the eyes of the white men on horse-back, but before he could re-act it was too late. The Indian felt the pressure of a gun barrel at the back of his scull followed by the clicking sound of a revolvers hammer. The Indian moved the knife slowly from Helens temple; when it was six inches from her head is when Bodie fired and shot the knife from the Indians hand and taking parts of two fingers. Blood splattered Helens face as Hunter yanked the red man off the back of his horse. Helen came with; somehow she managed a controlled fall and landed on her feet; she quickly turned toward them,

"Stop!" She yelled.

Hunter looked at her questionably.

"Don't kill him, we have killed enough of his people."

Hunter holstered his gun and just stood there, overshadowing the Indian who was in a sitting position and cradling his bloody fingers.

Helen took a bandana from her neck and bent down and wrapped the bewildered Seminole's hand.

"You were of the Snake Clan, yes?"

The Indian nodded his head with a slight understanding?

"Git up, git on your horse and move along. Go back to your people."

The Seminole Indian looked to the gunslinger; Hunter shook his head and waved his hand toward the man's horse and then pointed down the trail.

The rest maneuvered their horses to give the Seminole a path as he mounted his horse. As he rode past, Bird said to him, "Today is your lucky day Injun; best not show your face again."

Helen hugged and kissed Hunter. He looked at the others as they looked away embarrassed for him. They went through the short greetings and began removing the bodies from the trail. They found a clearing and burnt the bodies as was an approved ritual for the Natives.

Hunter walked down the trail a ways and whistled loud in three quick burst, and in within a minute Zeke and Mocha appeared with their greetings. No one was happier than Bird to see Mocha; he ran to meet her bent down to hug the chocolate lab, allowing her licks to cover his face.

Night was coming; further north they found a suitable clearing for a camp. Tonight they would celebrate their reuniting and plan their next move.

CHAPTER FOURTEEN

Hunter set out under the early morning moonlight to scout the location of Black Creek, while the others slept. He was surprised to see sawmills along the river of Clay County, telling him that they were further north than he had first thought. He rode back to camp as the sun began to rise. The camp was struck and the horses were saddled. All were sipping coffee and ready to ride.

"It's not much further now.' Hunter said as he climbed down from Zeke and joined Helen and the others at the fire. Jebidiah poured Hunter a tin of coffee and handed it to him. He nodded thanks and took a sip.

"Clay County is known for its lawlessness, every scoundrel this side of the Mississippi has a hide-out around in this area." Jebidiah said this while he blew smoke from his nostrils.

"That is why I need to stop here Jeb," said Hunter, "this would be a bounty hunters must stop for information."

"Makes sense," said Walt, "hell, even the armies don't set foot in Clay County."

"I heard the stories," said Bodie, "before the war a platoon of twenty bluecoats passed through here and was never seen again. They say the ones that refused to desert were tied to logs and run through a saw-mill."

Helen shivered a little, "and you were gonna ride in their by yourself?"

Hunter glanced at Helen over the rim of his coffee tin, "I figured I'd fit in just fine around here."

"We all ride in together or we turn around and go home." Helen said while standing up and resting her palm on the pistol butt of her dragoon.

Bird stood and began to pace as he spoke. "So we're just gonna ride in and take on anyone with a wanted poster; right out in the open in broad daylight?"

"That's exactly what we gonna do." Hunter said.

Walt let out a loud breath while opening a whiskey jar, he took a good swig; whiskey dripped from his whiskers.

"What the hell," Walt said, "I can't sing and I can't dance, and I sure as hell ain't gonna live forever; shit, might not even live out the day?"

"Walt!" said Jebidiah, "Can we be more on the positive please, I beg yah?"

"You two old coots." Said Bird under his breath but loud enough for all to hear.

"I know you heard this before," said Hunter, "this is my fight..."

Helen interrupted, "Stop right there, we ain't goin' through that again."

"One fight, we all fight." said Bodie.

"Do we have a plan, gunslinger?" asked Jebidiah.

"Much the same as all the others I expects."

"Huh, great!" said Walt as he took another swig.

"Ride in and kill them all." said Bird as he began to check his guns.

"Not all," said Hunter, "just the ones with posters on their person and bad intent in their look."

"What about Mocha?" Bird asked.

"She knows how to stay scarce when trouble hits." Hunter answered.

They went through the thorough check of their weapons and pulled extra ammunition from the saddle bags, placing bullets on their person for easy access. Bird kicked dirt on the fire as the others mounted up.

Bird fed Mocha jerky to keep her at the rear with him as they moved out. It would take little time to reach the mill town and would put them there early morning and giving them an edge. The saloons never closed and were well known for gambling late into the night. Facing men, drunk or hung over was always an advantage. The girls at the bordello would help catch them with their pants down. The Hunters of bounty would not expect the gunslinger to ride into town with a small army of friends.

There was nothing but the sound of hoofs clopping on the hard packed dirt as they slowly moved their horses down the main street. A woman stopped her sweeping of the porch at the feed store and watched them pass by. A young boy ran across the street from one building to another and paused to look at them before entering and then vanishing through the door. A dog barked as they passed; Mocha's ears went up but she kept moving alongside Birds horse. Hunter was leading the way with Helen by his side, they were two by two and heading for the saloon. It was early for such activity and people could be seen looking from windows and peeking through doors at the sounds of the horses entering the town.

Hunter and Helen dismounted first and tied their horses to the hitching post in the front of the saloon. The others were on alert; looking around high and low and watching their backs. As Hunter and Helen reached the bat wing doors, the gunslinger stopped and looked at the outside wall to see his wanted poster nailed there. He pulled it down with a yank and entered the saloon. Stopping inside the doors the gunslinger and Helen scanned the big rectangle shaped room searching for danger. To their left a young Spanish girl with a scared face swept the floor around a seated cowboy, he was passed out and face down on a table. To their right three men were playing cards far in the opposite corner, their backs to the wall. A large, hairy man behind the bar was wiping glasses with a rag. He did not take his eyes from them but moved from where he was and went to a spot at the middle of the bar; Hunter suspected he did this on purpose? His suspicions were verified when the bar keeps hand reached down below. The three men in the far off corner were watching them but continued drinking and dealing the cards.

Helen watched the three poker players and Hunter kept his eyes upon the bar-keep as they moved forward and toward the bar. Hunter noticed that the wood paneling at the center of the counter where the big man stood was discolored from the other planks. The outer bar wall had been fixed recently, Hunter knew from experience that a double barreled sawed of shot gun was most likely mounted there and aiming outward.

"Bottle," Hunter said as he tossed a gold coin on the counter. The bar-keep watched it as it spun and then settled to a stop.

"I don't got change this early." Said the big man, his voice was raspy and deep.

Hunter nodded his okay. The bar-keep turned and then came back with a bottle and two shot glasses. Hunter poured one glass and slid it toward Helen; she shook her head no as she was clearly on alert and watching the men in the corner. Hunter slammed back the whiskey and poured another and immediately slammed that one back. He left Helen's shot in case she changed her mind.

Hunter held up the poster he had plucked from the front of the building and struck a match; he lit the poster from his hand and laid it on the bars counter to burn. He spoke in a loud voice in making sure the three men gambling in the back could hear.

"Before you think about collectin' any bounty this day, I'll tell ya right now there ain't none. The printers and payers are dead, done private not by the government, There is no money."

"Is that so?" replied the bar-keep, "and why should any believe your word on it?"

"Would I walk in here like this if I were lyin'?"

"Maybe? You might be full of yourself or just plum loco, what do I care. I am a drink slinger not a gunfighter, but I'll tell ya there have been many bounty hunters come through here the last few months or so and most had that there picture."

"How many are still here?" asked Hunter.

"More than you and the lady here would want to take on, I can tell ya." When the bar-keep said this his eyes gave him away; he glanced over at the three men in the corner playing poker. Helen had been watching them while Hunter and the man conversed and she noticed the players were murmuring and were no longer playing their game but acting it out. She cocked one of her dragoons in its holster to warn Hunter. When she did this the barkeeps eyes gave him away once again and his arm reached down below the counter. Hunter grabbed Helen and yanked her as hard as he could and side stepping as the shot rang out and the wood from under the bar splintered outward just missing her. Hunter ignored the sting in the back of his leg as he pulled his pistol; the big man behind the bar brought the shot gun up and over the counter. He never got the second shot off before Hunter put two slugs in his chest. Smoke filled their end of the room. Helen had recovered and was back steady on her feet and firing at the men across the room stopping their forward progress. They had turned a table on its side for cover and were firing back. Hunter unloaded one revolver laying down cover for they were in the open. The three men were sliding the table forward to make an attack. Passing the front door was their last mistake; the table was protecting them from Helen and Hunters gun fire but they did not count on Walt and Jebidiah coming through the swinging doors at their flank and killing them dead. Two shots, one after the other of Walt's shot gun hurt the first two while Jebidiah's pistol fire finished the last.

"Well, the whole towns gonna wake now, best hunker down." Walt yelled out as he reloaded his scatter gun.

"Where's Bodie and Bird?" Helen asked loudly.

"They took the horses and the dog around back." Jebidiah answered.

"See if there is a back door to this place and git them inside.' Said Hunter as he checked his back leg where there was some blood, but it was just a scratch, a few led balls from the shotgun spray.

Jebidiah found a rear entrance and unlocked it. Mocha ran in followed by Bird and Bodie.

"This town is stirrin' up now." announced Bodie.

"Trapped like rats." Bird commented.

"Is there a window back there for lookin' out?" Hunter yelled.

"Yes, two small ones on each side of the door." Bodie answered through the inside doorway to the back room.

"We need somebody with a rifle to keep them off the horses." Hunter yelled back as he reloaded.

"I got it!" yelled Bird.

Hunter and Helen slid a table in front of the bat wing doors and tipped it on its side to block easy entry. Jebidiah and Walt were at the picture windows at the front looking out as the streets were coming alive with people. Hunter dug through the pockets of the dead men and found the wanted posters with his likeness on it. He also found one with the name and picture of Darnell upon it, the half Negro that killed his former master. Hunter stacked his posters on the bar and set a bottle on top. He then lit the Darnell poster with a match and dropped it to the floor.

"Why burn that one?" Helen asked.

"I knew the man he killed, he had it comin'."

"I got about ten men with guns out here takin' position!" Bodie yelled, as he carefully peered out one front window at the right of the doors. There were two large windows on each side of the front entrance separated by three feet of wall. Jebidiah and Walt were covering two on the left side and Hunter and Helen took position at the batwing doors. Helen was on one knee prepared to shoot her rifle over the table and under the right batwing. Hunter was standing and aiming over the left batwing. They all had repeating rifles, Walt had a long barrel shot gun leaning against the wall for back-up. They all had removed the saddle bags from the horses with their extra ammo, jerky and water. This standoff would not take long; it might be over in minutes depending on how bad the men of this town wanted the reward on the half-breed gunslinger.

"Bodie, you keep a good eye for any torches," Said Hunter, "if they decide to burn us out we're gonna have to shoot our way outta here quick."

"I'm gittin' too old for this shit." Walt commented.

"I got at the least two back here in the woods lurkin'!" yelled Bird from the back room.

"Give them some warnin'," Yelled Hunter, "if they go for the horses then shoot to kill."

Glass broke and Bird fired through a square window pane. He shot at the feet of one man making his way forward, the man ducked behind a tree and fired back; more glass shattered and Bird dipped back. Another man was coming forward over a small ditch between the saloon and the tree line. Bird shot him in the chest. The first man tried to get from one tree to another, but Bird fired his rifle and put him down. Bird studied the woods intently; he then spotted more movement among the brush.

"I got the two, but theres more comin'!" Bird yelled with excitement.

Hunter looked at Helen but before he could speak it she was on the move, "I got him."

She left Hunters side for the back room to help the boy protect the horses. Shots shattered the glass windows at the front on her retreat; Helen had to duck and dodge to avoid the bullets. After the first barrage of gun fire from the outside, Hunter, Bodie, Walt and Jebidiah opened up with their rifles. Unlike the men shooting up the building with no real target, Hunter and the boys had the shooters in clear sight, hiding behind rain barrels, a wagon, and some on the roof. There were a few men firing from the windows of the Hotel across the thirty foot wide street. Hunter killed a man who poked his head out from behind a wood barrel with a head shot. Jebidiah got one in the leg in-between the spindles of a wagon wheel. A body fell from the sky as Walt gut shot one on the roof. The bar was filling with smoke as the hammers on the rifles quickly clicked dry. They ducked down and began to reload as another barrage of bullets shattered wood and the remaining glass from the outside. The two booms from Walt's shot gun was heard and then rifle fire followed.

Shots could be heard firing from the back room. Hunter was relieved to hear the pitch of Helens baby dragoons; if her guns were firing then she was still on her feet. She was no doubt keeping the attackers at bay as Bird reloaded the rifles.

A body hit the street from above with a puff of dust as Jebidiah cleared another from the roof. Hunter was working the hotel windows trying to catch one out in the open. The glass on the building was about gone leaving only a few square pains. The hotel was three stories and then the roof. There were men on all three floors now; they were firing at the saloon. Some were hooting and hollering obviously still drunk from the night before. These men would not live through the day.

As quick as it started all firing suddenly stopped and the silence was deafening. The streets looked like the fourth of July after a fireworks show as the smoke rose into the morning sky.

Helen came to Hunters side from the back room. Hunter was kneeling behind the table and reloading the yellow Boy.

"The horses are good, four dead and the woods are clear for now. Bird is still on the lookout."

Hunter nodded and peeked out through the door to take a look.

Jebidiah sounded out, "Helen do you have some bandages?"

"Are you hit Jeb?"

"I'm good, Walt needs some tendin' to though."

Helen grabbed a bag and keeping low she went to the other side of the saloon to where Walt was watching the window. When he turned to her she saw a line of blood running down his face just below a chunk of glass that was protruding from his upper cheek and just below the eye.

"Were you just gonna leave that in there? Helen asked.

"I was," replied Walt, "until I had a rag, when this glass gits pulled it's gonna bleed like no one's business."

"How deep is it you figure?" asked Helen.

"I can feel it on the bone."

Helen slid a small table over to work on. She took some tobacco from a pouch and placed it in a bowl. She then poured a splash of whiskey in to wet it. Before she could set down the bottle, Walt stopped her.

"Ah,ah." Walt said with his arm outstretched. With a slight eye roll Helen handed him the bottle and he tipped it back several times as she mixed the tobacco and whiskey with her fingers and rolling a small amount into a sticky ball.

"Hold still." She said as she reached up pulled the glass; blood spurted but she quickly slapped a rag to it.

"You need stitchin'."

"Later," said Walt with a groan, "were a little busy right now."

Helen pulled away the rag and dropped it to the floor; she used both hands to apply the tobacco into the wound and pressing firmly. Walt moaned as it stung something awful.

"Now that's only gonna stay if you're careful."

"Hunter!" Jebidiah shouted out, "there's someone a comin', he's wearin' a star and he looks to be carrin' a parlay?"

Hunter pulled the sawed off shot gun from his side shoulder holster and stood at the center of the front bat wing doors. He peered out to see the man who had a piece of white sheet tied to his rifle. The man stepped up onto the porch a mere two feet away, just on the other side of the hanging doors and met Hunter eye to eye. The man with the tin star looked down to see the barrels of the shot gun aimed at his crotch just underneath the batwings.

"I need a word." said the lawman.

After a short stare down; Hunter then looked side to side and checking for any signs of a trick. Satisfied, Hunter backed up keeping the shotgun leveled.

"Come in but leave the rifle."

Jebidiah and Helen slid the table aside. The lawman leaned his rifle with the white rag tied to it against the outside of the building and entered through the swinging doors.

"That's far enough." said Hunter.

"The names Tobin, Texas Ranger."

"You're a long way from Texas mister; I do believe you are out of your jurisdiction?" Hunter questioned.

"I'm workin' as a bounty hunter these days, pay for a Ranger ain't too good and what there is of it is slow comin'."

"Well there ain't no fool's gold." Said Jebidiah, with his revolver aimed at the man's head.

"That's why I come here like this," said the Ranger, "Jane Montgomery has gone missin' for a long time now. All her wealth and assets has been stole or confiscated by the banks, she is believed to be dead. I received a telegram on this just yesterday."

"Then why is you still here lawman?" said Walt, walking into the rangers view from the corner of the room.

"I was headed out of town this mornin', until you all showed. I told many here of what I had learned..."

"But they didn't believe ya did they?" interrupted Hunter.

"No they did not; they figured I was lyin' to get to the reward money for myself, thin out the herd so to speak, either way some would just assume kills ya out of sheer boredom."

"And what would you assume, Mr. Tobin?" Helen asked.

"My horse is done packed ma'am, I am movin' on."

The Ranger asked Hunter's permission with a look as he made a move for the inside pocket of his duster. Hunter nodded yes; allowing him to pull a paper from his pocket. The Ranger unfolded it and placed it on a table just to his right, the picture was face up for all to see Hunters likeness.

"Good luck." Said Tobin, He tipped his hat as he back out of the saloon through the swinging doors. Bodie stepped up and slid the turned table back to block the bottom of the doorway.

"Well that's one dangerous man disarmed, but there's still about ten more out there that needs killin'." As soon as Bodie said this the bullets began to fly, splintering wood and breaking the last of the glass.

He went low and ran from the doorway as they all took up their positions and waiting for a break to fire back. It suddenly got quiet while the attackers reloaded.

Hunter spoke out. "Hold up, save the ammo, pick a target and wait until they peer out for the next barrage, and make the shot count."

Bird yelled out from the back room, "I got more in the woods back here!" followed by his rifle fire.

"I got it." Helen sounded out as she headed for the back and moving low.

As soon as the people of the town left their cover to shoot they were immediately fired upon by the waiting James boys. The timing worked perfectly; Walt, Jebidiah, and Bodie hit their targets. Some wounded and some killed. Hunter killed two in two different windows, both head shots, one through the teeth.

A man came out of the front door of the hotel with a stumbling limp and a wanted poster waving in his hand like a white flag. His leg was bleeding and he had one hand applying pressure on a shoulder wound.

"Hold your fire!" yelled the man, "I'm done here, I need the Doc."

The man clumsily went to one knee and set the wanted poster on the front steps and set his revolver on top to keep the wind from blowing it away.

A man who was apparently the town Doctor showed himself with a youngster by his side. They helped the wounded man up to his feet and quickly carted him down the road.

Helen came back into the room announcing as she re-loaded,

"The horses are safe, some dead and some fled, and Bird says let's git this over with cause he's gittin' hungry."

Walt suddenly yelled out questionably from his view at one front window, "I don't see noone out there. This shit might be over?"

"All clear at this end." Bodie said from his view.

"Not so fast." Hunter said as peered over the swinging bat-wing doors.

They all looked with caution, some from the window and Helen over Hunters shoulder. Exiting the hotel was a big man with a scruffy beard that grew in different directions guided by the scares on his face. Hunter noticed he moved smooth like liquid, which looked strange for such a large man. He was dirty and backwoods looking. His hat and cloths were worn showing signs of many days on the trail. His gun was a single shooter, a shiny 45 with nickel plate in a holster built for speed draw.

"It's just you and me now half-breed," yelled the gunman from where he stopped in the street holding a poster high in his hand. "You want it come and get it."

"You gonna surrender that wanted poster?" Hunter yelled back.

"I gonna collect on it, you ain't no Wild Bill Hickok half-breed."

"How bout I just shoot this SOB right now?" Bodie said with his rifle aimed out his window.

"No Bode," commanded Hunter, "I've been called out and I tend to finish this. Collect the horses, mount up and wait for me at the end of the street."

Helen came forward to face the gunslinger, "You listen here Hunter James Dolin, you shoot to kill; you hear me? And then were done here, we go home, promise me?"

He was checking his pistols as she talked. He then looked at her.

"The only thing I can promise is we will head south, what happens between here and home, I cannot say."

Jebidiah walked forward, "You watch yourself son, I think I might know of this man and do not take him lightly, he's a big one, and it might take more than one bullet to put him down?"

Hunter nodded his understanding and headed for the door.

Walt walked up and gave Hunter a pat on the back, "You be as careful as the naked man climbin' a barbed-wire fence, you hear me?"

"I think I hear what your sayin' Walt?"

Hunter slid the table away from the batwings and walked through. Bodie cocked his rifle and went to the window. "This will be a fair fight I'll see to it."

"Hunter wanted us to mount up Bodie." Helen said.

"I'll be right behind ya, take my horse and I will catch up, one way or the other."

Bird entered the room from the back and went to another window.

"Take my horse too," said Bird, then cocking his rifle, "when this is over we will collect the gunslinger and meet up with ya."

Bodie nodded at the boy and decided not to argue with him. Bird was a man now and it was time he started treating him like one.

Hunter walked to the middle of the road and faced the man who waited with his right hand, high and flat on his belly. The single revolver was horizontal in a short holster at his mid-section. This was a practiced technique. Hunter removed his suede jacket and dropped it to the ground and took his stance.

The gunfighter held up the wanted poster and showed it to Hunter as if to justify his actions.

"There ain't no bounty, I killed the author of that post." Hunter said.

With a smirk the man crumbled up the paper and dropped it to the ground.

"I believe ya half-breed, but it don't matter none now, I came all this way from as far as Northern Kentucky. I heard over and over of the half-breed gunslinger that everyone's so scared of, well, I'm tired of hearin' it."

Hunters reply was only silence. Both men's eyes squinted with concentration which seemed to stop time. Any sounds around them were totally blocked out as the seconds ticked by... Bodie and Bird unwillingly held their breath as they watched Hunters back from the saloon window.

Some would later say that the bounty hunter had drawn first but Hunter was so fast to his movements they could not be sure. Puffs of smoke followed the loud bangs as the bounty hunter went down on both knees, Hunter landed on his back and his hat flew off; his head was bleeding but he was still moving as he rolled on his front side and managed to get to one knee. Hunter's vision was blurry and blood covered one eye completely. He suddenly realized his back was to the gunfighter. Hunter heard the click of a revolver behind him, with more reaction than thought he spun on one knee in the direction of the sound and using his memory of the man's placement. Hunter slammed the hammer down again and again unloading his revolve. The bounty hunter got off one shot from his kneeling position and missed. Two of Hunters 44's hit the big man in the chest, just above a hole in his gut where Hunters first draw had hit; this put the big man down for good. Hunter went down face first and everything went black.

People slowly began entering the street from behind their closed doors. Bodie and Bird ran from the saloon to Hunters side with their rifles at the ready. Bird covered as Bodie went to one knee and turned the gunslinger over. The bullet had grazed his scalp and there was blood everywhere. His hair would not ever lay the same and his head would probably hurt for a while, but it was not a significant wound.

"Bode, we got company." Bird warned.

Three armed men and one that was dressed like the undertaker gathered around the bounty hunters dead body only. A grey haired man carrying a medical bag ran over to Hunter and kneeled to check his head.

"You need to git him off the street," said the Doc as he pressed his fingers to Hunters wound, "The three men there are somewhat friendly with the deceased, his name was Jim Callahan."

The three men fanned out and started to move forward to face them; Bodie and Bird raised their rifles as the air thickened with tension. The men suddenly stopped in their tracks as the clopping sounds of hooves rode up behind Bodie and Bird. Jebidiah and Walt had their rifles leveled and all the horses in tow. Helen jumped from her mount and went to Hunter. He began to wake with a slight moan as Mocha licked the blood from his face.

"He will live ma'am, might have one hell of a headache though?" said the doc.

"Alright dog," said Hunter as he sat up to avoid the dogs tongue.

Helen and the Doc helped Hunter to his feet.

"I'm fine," Hunter said "let us finish this and move the hell out."

"Finish what?" asked Jebidiah from the back of his horse."

Hunter turned and spoke to him,

"I want all the posters in this town."

"I'm gittin too old for this shit!" exclaimed Walt.

"Shut it Walt," said Jebidiah, "son, we been lucky to this point...."

Before Jebidiah could finish his point, a boy ran up to Hunter and handed him a messy stack of posters, and then ran off. Hunter looked to see the remaining three gunmen walking away.

"Can we head home now please?" begged Helen, as she handed Hunter his hat.

He stuck his finger in a hole of his Stetson, "I'm gonna need a new hat."

"We will, in the store of the next town please." Helen pleaded.

The James family rode south west leaving Black Creek behind. Hunter was satisfied that he had destroyed a good amount of the wanted posters with his likeness upon it. He was satisfied enough that he could go back to Myakka and wait on any stragglers that would hunt him down and try him. Some would come just to prove they were faster and more deadly than the gunslinger. When he had first set out to collect the posters, the idea was to remove any threat, so he and his family would not be looking over their shoulders for the rest of their days. Hunter realized he had been on a fool's errand for he would always have to watch his back to pay for the sins of his past. Hunter still planned on stopping in every town and every saloon from here to Myakka City to check for bounty hunters holding papers. This thought he kept to himself for now.

Chapter Fifteen

Captain William B. Hooker had sent men to search for Jimbo, Daryl and the half-breed when he received word they had not arrived at Fort Foster. The men found the bodies and brought them back for burial. Hooker knew he had made a mistake by underestimating the gunslinger. He did not care much for Daryl but Jimbo was a good man and had been with him for over ten years. Jimbo was a man the Captain could hold a quick conversation with, which was far and in-between out here in these parts.

Over time, Hooker had figured out that Hunter James was wanted not by the authorities but by questionable peoples, but the killing of Jimbo soured his stomach. The letter he had received from Jimbo's mother hit him deep, she had begged him for vengeance, and he had given her his word on a return letter. He would not hunt the gunslinger but if he ever came across him again he would feel compelled to act?

Chapter Sixteen

The James Family rode south for many days with the gunslinger leading the way. All was quiet; to their surprise they did not run across anyone searching for Hunter. Maybe the word got out that the hunters had become the hunted? Maybe that's all there was?

While stopping to water the horses, Helen made her way over to Jebidiah's side for she had just realized where they were.

"Tell me Jeb, is it just me or are we south of Myakka and headin' somewhere definite?"

"You would be right little lady, we are far south but as to where we are goin' I could not say."

Helen walked over to Hunter where he was squatting at the lakes edge and filling his canteen. She bent her knees by his side but said nothing; there was a long quiet pause.

"Somthin' on your mind little lady?" Hunter asked.

"What makes you say that?"

"Your silence screams louder than words."

There was another long quiet pause between them, before Helen continued.

"These men will follow you to the ends of the earth without question Hunter James; I on the other hand am a woman and I must know what's goin' on at all times, and I need to know before we go any further."

"Your right," he said, "you bein' kept in the dark was not my intention."

Hunter stood and began to speak, "I have one more stop to make, it seems that Captain Hooker has somethin' that belongs to me and I intend to git it back."

"The tomahawk," stated Helen.

Hunter nodded, "I'm not sure what has become of it but I'm' sure as hell gonna ask him."

"It is there, I saw it was mounted over his front door." Helen revealed.

"Pardon me for ear-droppin'" said Walt, "you killed two of his men, and I don't think he might be too kindly to see ya?"

Hunter then realized that everyone was there gathered around, and all had heard what he and Helen had been discussing.

"Well this is where we part ways then..." before Hunter could finish, they were all shaking their heads and speaking up.

"There's no way..." said Jebidiah.

"Again with this..." said Walt?

"I'm not leavin' your side..." said Helen.

"Seperatin's not a good idea..." said Bodie.

"I ain't afraid of them cow pokes..." said Bird.

"Ruff, ruff, ruff..." said Mocha.

"Alright, alright, you all are the most stubborn I ever did run across." Hunter said, as he quieted them down with his hands up.

"We got a plan son?" Jebidiah asked.

"Not really." Hunter answered.

"I'm still too old for this shit!" Walt muttered, as they mounted up and prepared to ride.

By the end of the day they would arrive just on the outside edge of Hookers land, and then onto the ranch where this whole thing started. Hooker had an estimated thirty ranch hands, twenty of them would be a force to reckon with, armed men protecting their livelihoods. Cracker cowboys were a tough breed and some of them where survivors of the Civil war, one of the bloodiest wars in history. Some of the older men fought in the third Seminole Indian War, some fought in all. Hunter did not want bloodshed, all he wanted was his tomahawk returned; if Hooker were to give it up there would be none.

On the edge of the woods Hunter looked around the pasture through the telescope searching for cowhands among the herd. He also searched for any bulls that may be in the field. The cows were grazing and some of the younger calves pranced, and then there was a bull but he was on the far side of the meadow and away from where they were heading. There were no cracker cowboys in sight; they most likely were headed for the bunk house at this time of the day. The horses would be brushed, fed and watered before the men would eat their last meal of the day.

Hunter decided to hunker down for the night and ride in at daybreak. Mayhem was not what he sought and moving in at night would be seen as an attack. There would be no fire for them, this close to the ranch the smoke could be smelled and the flame could be seen. Jerky and whiskey would be the meal for tonight and sleeping in shifts. The plan was to ride in early morning and ask Hooker to return Hunters property. If that did not work the tomahawk would have to be taken by force. This was more than about property, it was about honor. You did not call a man a liar or a cheater, and thieves were shot and or hanged by the nearest wood.

Helen had told Hunter that when she and little James were leaving the ranch she had seen the tomahawk mounted over the front door. Why not move in under the cover of darkness and steal it, and then move on, she had asked. Hunter said that would feel like thieving or coward's play and he would not be accused of either. How can steel something that is already yours, she had asked. He did not have an answer for her; just a look that said the conversation was over.

Hunter closed his eyes for some time but he did not sleep. The anticipation of what was to come with the early morn would not leave his mind. Bodie and Bird took first shift and Walt and Jebidiah took the last. They mounted up an hour before the sun and rode in as quiet and cautious as possible. They did not expect a lookout for this was a working ranch and far enough away from Indian Territory. The last thing Hooker would expect this morning was an army of gunfighters at his door.

The sun just began to show itself on the horizon when the cook came out of the front door with a pot in his hands. He did not look up until he slung the water onto the ground. He froze as he found himself in front of a line of horses about ten feet from the porch; his pot water hit the ground somewhere in the middle directly in front of the gunslinger. The splash up came dangerously close to the Appaloosa's hooves. The cook was wearing his faded red one piece underwear with boots and a single revolver hung from his hip. The first thought that crossed his mind was to drop the pot and draw, but when he looked into the steel blue eyes of the gunslinger he decided against it.

"I need to speak with Hooker." Hunter said.

"What fir?" The cook asked. He still had not moved in the slightest.

Hunter nodded high toward the door behind him, "I came for my property there, hanging just above your head."

The cook turned his head and body slow, to see the tomahawk mounted over the front door. He had seen it there before but he had paid no mind to it until now. "Well why don't you just take it and git before the boys wake, I won't speak a word."

"This ain't no robbery," said Hunter, "I expect it returned with an apology by Hooker, and then we will move on."

The cook's eyes went wide and he gave a laugh that sounded more like a grunt.

"Captain Hooker aint the apologizin' type which I have ever heard? You sure you want to war over some Injun's trinket?"

"I'll have what's mine one way or the other." Hunter replied.

The cook glanced up at the dinner bell that was mounted to the porches roof post. He peered at it for only a split second, but that was long enough to where it was noticed by all.

"Bird," said Hunter, "you want to get the man's gun and then hit that bell?"

Bird slid down from his horse and walked to the porch. Mocha went with him and stood and growled at the cook as if to guard him while Bird lifted the revolver. Bird went to the bell and grabbed the leather that hung from it. He looked at the gunslinger who then nodded; Bird produced a grin like a mischievous child as he then rang the bell several times and then several more.

Within minutes men began to appear from the house dressing and strapping on gun belts. Some looked annoyed and some looked confused. Bird walked quickly to his horse and mounted; pulling his revolver he turned with Bodie to cover some men coming from the barn at their rear. Bodie cocked the Winchester rifle and held it at the ready. Walt had the long barrel shotgun raised, Helen had pulled a pistol and Jebidiah cocked his rifle. Only the gunslinger did not draw.

Four men were lurking on the grounds and five men joined the cook on the front porch. They fanned out and faced Hunter and his crew.

"Keep movin' around front here where we can see yah." Bodie demanded as he raised the rifle to the men coming from the barn. They slowly moved to the flank and then joined the others on the ground in front of the porch. Hunter and his crew backed their horses up slowly to give more room. Nine men were fanned out and facing the gunslinger and his crew. They had their hands on the butts of their guns but not one dared to draw just yet.

"Where's the Captain?" Hunter asked.

"I'm here gunslinger." Said a voice from the open doorway as Hooker appeared. He was fully dressed unlike some of his men who were barefooted, some had suspenders hanging and one was in his under-garb but they all had brought their weapons.

"You should not have come back here Dolin." Hooker said.

"I've come for my property." Hunter's eyes glanced over Hooker's head where the Tomahawk was mounted. The Captain did not turn; he knew what was there for he had hung it himself.

"The best I can do is to bury you with it for I made a promise to Jimbo's mama who you killed."

"I had no choice," said Hunter, "He was taking me to hang."

"Jimbo was a good man and a friend, you should have let him live."

"It was him or me." Hunter replied. "If it makes you feel any better I liked the man for the short time I known him."

"Well it don't! And you're outnumbered."

"We are that," Hunter said, "but my people have been doing this for a long time, and I promise you will be the first to go."

Everyone tensed up on both sides from this talk.

"Boys, I know you ain't the type to shoot a woman but this one is a killer and her gun is out of her holster, when the shooting starts I want her to go down first."

Hookers order revealed his men's intentions. Hunter saw the look in the eyes of some who would not shoot even an armed woman, but three or four of these men would not hesitate to shoot Helen down. *This Captain is smart which makes him very dangerous,* thought Hunter, *I will not risk her.*

"I got this," whispered Helen to Hunter, "You do what you got to do."

"I don't want any of my family killed caused by me," announced Hunter, "and I would bet you don't want your men dead for a promise that you made to save face, so I'm calling you to the street Hooker, just you and me and the rest walk. What do you say?"

"Ha!" laughed the Captain, "You want me to draw down on the Half-breed Gunslinger, the fastest gun known in these parts. A known savage that has killed Indians, bounty hunters, and the whole Montgomery family while at the same time avoidin' capture by the Union Army, more than once. I'm no coward, but I do have the sense God gave me."

"Then were at a standoff it seems Captain."

"No, I think I have the upper hand, you surrender yourself and I will allow your crew safe passage."

"That's not gonna happen Hooker," said Jebidiah with conviction, "You know me, you know Walt, we ain't never run from a fight and we damn sure won't start now."

"So if you all are done jawin'" Interrupted Walt, "lets git with it."

There was a long pause and the air was thick with pressure. Hooker's men were getting antsy. They did not like the fact that their guns were still holstered. All it would take is a pull of a trigger to get Hooker's men to draw and Bird was about to do just that for he was young and impatient. Just then galloping hooves caught everyone's attention. Two of Hooker's men came in riding hard from the south field, they were yelling!

"What is it Jake?" asked the Captain?

One man on the horse talked through heavy breathe, "Renegades, they came in through the south swamp, they killed little Tommy Captain."

The other man continued on as the one caught his breath, "Got Tommy with an arrow in the back, they ambushed us, came out of nowhere."

"How many?" asked the Captain?

"Five, maybe ten, don't know for sure?"

"What about my cows?"

"I'm sorry sir we had to leave um, there were just too many."

Hunter suddenly thought there might be a way out of this mess. Nothing brings white men to the same side more than an Indian attack.

"Captain," interrupted Hunter, "I have some of the best Indian fighters here at my side, we can help you with the renegades, and then maybe you owe me somethin'?"

Hooker paced back and forth on his porch as he talked, "And what will be owed to you gunslinger?"

"Our lives and my tomahawk will be the price."

"My word is my creed to the old woman," Hooker said, "but my cows and my ranch and my men are my life. You help us kill the savages and retrieve any of my herd, and you got yourself a deal."

"Alright then," said Hunter, "Jeb, what do you think?"

"They came in from the south swamp; that is where we start. They will return the way they know and there is plenty of dry pasture beyond the bog."

"Walt?" asked Hunter.

"We split up and ride wide to the East and to the West rims, try to flank them then surround um."

"Good," replied Hunter, "While we ride the rims, Captain, you and your men ride up the middle and track them down, but don't go in to soon, you have to give us time to get in behind them and cut off any retreat."

The Captain nodded in agreement, "remember the cows are the most important, then the killing of the Injuns."

"Jeb you ride with me and Helen to the West side," said Hunter, "Walt you go with Bodie and Bird to the East."

While Hunter spoke his crew moved their horses into their groups of three preparing to move out. Mocha stood in the middle looking from one group to another as if deciding who to follow. She watched Bird as he began to move and then decided to follow Helen at the last minute. Hunter watched Mocha as she made her decision; he could not help grinning as he realized Helen now carried the saddle bag with the jerky.

Captain Hooker and his men hurried to prepare their horses and pack their gear. Hunter and his people needed some time to catch the Renegades and get in position on their flanks, so they rode out not waiting on the cracker cowboys.

They all rode together with Walt and Jebidiah leading and tracking the unshod horses. After a time the swamp grew thick and the trail more treacherous. The renegades were on a trail of dry land that weaved through the marsh. Hunter and his crew stayed together until they came out on the other side of the swamp were high ground lay. The raiding party was close now so Hunter took the time to stop everyone and water the horses. The day was warming fast and the humidity was high. Mocha drank from the marsh with the horses while the men and Helen drank from their canteens.

"This is where we split" said Hunter as he checked his weapons. "We Ride hard and flank them from both sides and then we meet up at their front. Keep your distance, it's crucial they don't know your there until we meet up in the middle."

"Then what?" asked Bird.

"We open fire on um, they will turn and retreat and run right into Hookers men."

"Well what are we waiting for, lets git this over with." Walt said.

Hunter had pulled his spy glass from his bag and was looking back for Captain Hooker and his men. They were riding hard but had a good distance to cover.

"There comin'," said Hunter, "Head out, flank the perimeter and when the renegades are sighted ride hard and out and up ahead to close off their route."

Walt, Bodie and Bird rode north /east and the gunslinger, Helen and Jebidiah took to the west side. Mocha started beside Helen and then soon took the lead following her nose.

The renegades were ten strong and moving slow, pushing only three cows for higher ground. The further away from the ranch they got, the more confident they were that no one followed. The Indians had not eaten meat in six days and they were desperate. They had been scavengers for so long the thought of hunting had left them and taking from others was now their way.

Mocha was running hard for some time when she suddenly stopped and veered to her left with a low guttural growl.

Hunter pulled Zeke's reins and circled back to the dog. Helen and Jebidiah followed.

"Easy girl, what is it?" He said.

Hunter opened the scope and began to scan through the trees that were numerous on the higher slope. The raiding party had stopped; He could see one Indian starting a fire as two others slit the throat of one of the cows. Hunter lowered the glass and sighed with a look of concern that Helen saw.

"What is it?" asked Helen, "What do you see?"

"These are not renegades; they are young Seminoles, ones that rode for White Owl, they appear to be starving."

"That ain't gonna matter much to Hooker and his men," Said Jebidiah, "cattle russlin' is a hangin' offense."

"Yep," said Hunter as he put the scope away. "We stick to the plan for now."

They rode north for a while and then circled to meet up with Walt, Bodie and the kid. Hunter wanted to get to the Seminoles first before The Captain and his men; that would be the young Indians only chance.

Hunter and his crew met up quickly, north of the Indians as they had stopped to butcher and eat one of the cows. For them to do this so close to the crime scene was a sign of desperation. Surrounding the Indians and killing them would be easy compared to what Hunter felt he must do, and that was save the young warriors. They had already killed a white man, one of Hookers ranch hands and now they had killed a cow; that debt would have to be paid.

"I see that look on your face Hunter James," said Jebidiah, "A dead cattleman, stolen cows from private land and one butchered, I see no way out for them but death?"

"What are we doin'?" asked Walt as he came along side.

"They're not renegades, they're young braves some as young as eighteen or so, if one is twenty I'd eat my hat." Hunter answered.

"A coming to manhood tradition for young Seminole warriors," continued Walt, "the tribe sends them out to hunt and survive. They must bring back the fur of a black bear, the head of a bald eagle and the tail of a panther before their return. I don't think cows are on the list?"

"No that aint it," replied Hunter, "These young braves are scattered because Helen and me killed their leader. Going back to the Snake Clan may have not been an option for them."

"What are we gonna do?" asked Bodie, "kill Hooker and his men, the Captain is well known and liked, the army would be down here before you could digest and spit out that hat."

"I don't know yet?" replied Hunter, "but getting to the Seminoles first could be a big help."

"What if we could stall Hooker somehow?" suggested Bird.

"What do you got in mind kid?" asked Walt.

"I saw a huge hornets nest a little ways back on the trail at the fork, a low hanging branch, it would sure scatter um about."

"Alright Bird," said Hunter, "do it, we don't have much time."

Bird took off back to the path, the same direction they had just come from. He had to reach the place where they changed direction before Hooker and his men did. He had to set up the diversion without getting attacked himself by the stinging army.

He made it to the tree that held the nest and climbed it. Hunter had given Bird the spy glass for which he used now. There was no sign of Hooker and his men on the trail but he felt he must hurry. Bird slid out onto the branch with a small bone saw in hand and twenty feet of rope. He tied the rope to the smaller branch that the hornets' nest was attached to; he then sawed carefully at the branch. Bird was careful only to saw half-way through and trying not to disturb the nest until ready. Hornets buzzed around as the sawing motion shook the nest. They had not found him for he was a good four feet above the hive but they were getting angry and swarming below. He tied the rope to the branch that held the nest just below the cut.With the rope sliding in his loosely closed fist he crawled backwards along the branch to the base of the tree and then onto another branch on the other side of the trunk. Here he waited.

Ten minutes later he heard the hooves before he saw the men moving quick and coming toward him on their horses. Timing would be everything for this to work; too late and they would ride by, too soon and they could stop and change direction only stalling their progress for a short time.

Bird's hands clenched tight around the rope as he waited; he judged the distance and then pulled, the branch made a cracking sound and snapped; the nest hit the ground in the middle of the trail and broke apart. The Hornets went crazy directly in front of the men and their steeds. The flying army spread out in their attack like a tornado. Hooker and his men pulled back on the reins and began to scatter; the horses where neighing in a panic and bumping off of each other. They turned and rode back down the trail with a stream of hornets chasing them.

Bird was already on the move and hanging from a branch, he dropped onto his gelding, and reeling the rope in. Luckily the hornets' nest had broken in half and come loose from the branch. A small amount of hornets buzzed him but the majority where chasing down Hooker and his men. He spurred his horse into a run. They would have to take another trail which would delay them for at the least 45 minutes. Hopefully that would be enough time for the gunslinger to do whatever he was going to do.

Chapter Seventeen

Hunter walked into the center of their camp with his guns holstered. Several of the young warriors were quickly on him with rifles. In an instant cocking sounds of rifles and clicking sounds of triggers could be heard as the James crew appeared from the brush and into the clearing; they surrounded the young braves. Walt had his double barrel shot gun, Bodie and Jebidiah had rifles and Helen had both pistols drawn. The young Indians looked shocked and then nervous but kept their weapons leveled at the gunslinger.

"I hope you'll speak English 'cause my Creek is rusty at best." Hunter said.

He spoke directly to two of the slightly older Seminoles that he expected one was the leader of this rabble.

"In about thirty minutes there'll be half a dozen cowboys riding up that trail..."

Hunter was interrupted by Bird's horse riding in hard and into the clearing.

"More like twenty minutes there, boss." Bird said, with short breath. He pulled his pistol and cocked the hammer pointing it at the head of an Indian that held a rifle on the gunslinger.

Hunter continued, "Here's the deal, leave the cows and ride on hard and fast or you will die here, don't ever come back."

"Why do this?" asked the leader of the young Creeks, one that was closest to Hunter.

"The killin' needs to stop sometime, maybe this is a good time and place as any?"

The brave lowered his rifle and nodded to the rest. They lowered their weapons and began moving for their horses cautiously. Walt and Jebidiah backed away slowly to give them room but neither lowered their guns.

"I advise you to take to the swamp, less chance they will follow you through there."

With a nod to the gunslinger the Indian braves rode on quickly, the direction they took would put them into some of the deepest swamp in this area, heeding the gunslingers advice.

"Now what?" asked Bird as he dismounted his steed?

"We wait." Hunter answered.

"Shit! Hooker ain't gonna be too happy we let um go." Walt said.

"We didn't let um go Walt," replied Hunter "we were too late and they were gone before we got here. They left the cattle and ran; hooker will just have to except it?"

Hunter checked the terrain looking for Hooker and his men with the scope he retrieved from Bird. When there was no sign he decided to clean up the slaughter of the cow. The Indians took the meat with them but let the carcass lay. Hooker would be more apt to go after the Indians if he saw the dead cow than if one was just missing.

The fire was put out and the carcass was buried in the thicket. They tried to make the camp look more occupied than it was as if the braves cut out for the swamp hours ago. Just as they were finishing up the sound of horses riding could be heard, getting louder by the second. They rode in with Hooker leading the way. Bird tensed up, for he didn't know for sure if he had been spotted while molesting the hornets' nest.

The James family was prepared in their minds for a shootout if their plan of deceit failed.

The first thing Helen noticed was the puffiness on some of the cowboys faces from what could only be hornet stings. They looked beat up and sick.

"Where the Hell is they Gunslinger?" Hooker demanded.

"Gone," said Hunter, "tracks lead deep into the swamp, maybe an hour or two ahead?"

"You let them git away!" he yelled.

"Let nothin', we're hunting Creek Indians in the land of their ancestors, they were runnin' scared, sometimes the rabbit out runs the coyote."

One of Hookers men fell from his saddle and hit the ground with a moan. His face was swollen and red. Two of the men dismounted and helped him back on his horse.

"Run into some trouble on the trail?" asked Bird, who got a sharp suspicious look from Hooker.

One of the cowboys spoke up, "We ran across a hornets nest, the biggest I'd ever saw. Captain I don't feel too good."

"They left the cows behind Captain," said Jebidiah, "not a total loss, your men are sick and I think we did honor our agreement?"

Captain Hooker rubbed a sting on his neck; his anger calmed to a sigh.

"Round up them cow's boys were done here." Hooker ordered this and then he pulled the tomahawk from his waist band and tossed it to Hunter. Hunter caught it and in one motion slid it into his belt.

Helen let out her air as she realized she was holding her breathe for some time. Bird had a grin on his face that would not stop. Walt pulled a draw from his bottle and Mocha barked at the cows as the cowboys guided them away.

"I expect we won't see you in these parts anytime soon gunslinger." Hooker commented.

"No I reckin' not Captain."

"If you're ever near Myakka City Captain, swing on by for a drink, on the house." said Jebidiah.

"We don't git north much old timer." The Captain rode out of the clearing with his cattle and his men. They were a tough lot but looking ragged and whooped. As soon as they were out of ear shot, Bird's grin turned to laughter. Soon they were all laughing at the thought of grown men on the run flailing and swatting at the flying army of hornets.

Chapter Eighteen

The four days ride home was uneventful putting them just outside Myakka City at mid- morning. The James family was tired and feeling good about getting home when Hunter suddenly pulled back on the reins and threw up a fist, stopping Zeke and slowing the rest to a halt. They were on the road that led into their town. Hunter stared at the old sign posts and the downed wood that once read Myakka City. Through the vinery growth Hunter thought he could just make out the cut from his bowie knife that crossed out the population number making it zero. It seemed so long ago when the gunslingers little war had begun, and perhaps it was.

"Home sweet Home," Walt said as he spit chaw juice to the ground.

"I for one am glad to be home." Helen said with some relief.

"Folks," said Bodie, "I hate to break up this reunion, but what is that all about you think?" he pointed up to the sky over the town where white smoke bellowed.

"What in the Hell?" said Walt, "That's still smoke; I shut it down when we left, someone is cooking corn."

Hunter immediately began the process of checking his guns. The rest followed his lead and doing the same. The sound of metal clicking and levers locking went on for a minute. Zeke's head bobbed up and down as she neighed making the other horses restless, for they knew trouble always followed the metal gun sounds. Hunter turned Zeke around with a pull on the reins so he was facing the others, before he spoke.

"Me, Bodie and Bird are gonna ride in at the front; Helen you take Walt and Jeb come in through the field behind Mat's. Let us engage first and see what's what; you three hang back and flank us if there is trouble, any questions?"

No one said a word; they just shook their heads in agreement.

Well I'll be damned!" Hunter said, looking around from one to the other, "No arguments? That's a first; someone should write this down and date it."

There were grins and snickers.

Walt spoke out, "We're just good to have some sorta plan going in, for a change."

They moved out down the road to confront who ever may have taken up residence in their town.

Hunter, Bodie and Bird rode their horses at a walk, three abreast as they entered Myakka. The town was in full function. There were two large wood covered wagons parked outside the barn. They had a costly look and were fortified like the ones used by Wells Fargo to transport money out in the west. But these were more on the fancy side with curtains and colored paint. The barn doors were opened and the back end of the pulling horses could be seen.

There were people coming and going from the hotel to the saloon. Some of them were locals and when they saw the gunslinger riding into town, some mounted their horses and rode out; others ducked back into the hotel and could be seen peering out the windows. Bessie appeared looking over the bat wing doors of the hotel and nodded her head toward the saloon when Hunter noticed her. He did not tip his hat or give away her acknowledgement as she disappeared back inside the building.

Hunter, Bodie and Bird dismounted and tied their horses to the hitching post outside Mats place. There was no talk; Bodie and Bird would follow Hunters lead as usual, there was no real plan other than shoot when shot at.

With his hands on the top of the batwing doors, Hunter peered inside allowing his eyes to adjust to the darkness. His hat was set low to cover his identity for as long as possible. A quick scan of the saloon showed Hunter there were possible friendlies inside, Cracker cowboys that had backed the gunslingers play before. The other half was men with blue coats and red legs. The bartender was a big man with a long red beard and a slashing scar that covered his cheek. Hunter spotted a man sitting at one of the two far tables at the back of the room. His blue coat was that of a Colonel. He had long white hair and a white mustache that went straight down on both sides and past his chin. This man was clearly the leader of this rabble. The fact that this man still wore his stripes on his uniform so long after the end of the war, said much about his demeanor.

Hunter entered the saloon as the barkeep walked to the far end of the bar and turned toward the table were the Colonel sat; Hunter stopped in the gunslingers stance, leaving his coat over the butts of his revolvers. Bodie and Bird fanned out by his side, one to the left and one to the right one step behind him. They threw their coat flaps aside and rested their hands on their pistols. The door to Mats was at the west end of the building and the Colonel and his men were seated at the East end, in the middle were a half dozen Cracker Cowboys and two local girls sitting on their laps. The dozen men in blue were strategically seated at the back with the possible friendlies in-between them. The locals would think twice about joining in the fight if they were caught in the crossfire.

The room was suddenly filled with the sound of chairs sliding on the wood floor as the red legs stood from their card tables.

"Easy there boys." The Colonel said from his seated position. He lowered his hand that held the five playing cards and lifted his head. Under the rim of his Colonels hat his eyes were dark and filled with deadly experience, there was no fear there. The Cracker Cowboys froze as they realized they were caught in the middle.

"You gals scoot on outta here." Hunter said.

The girls looked to the Colonel; He stood slow and made a gesture with his head which sent them scrambling out the door. The local boys were looking anxious.

"You cracker boys stay put and don't make a move or my men will cut you down," warned the Colonel, "That goes the same for you and your men half-breed."

"Your trespassin' red leg." Hunter replied."

"I claimed an abandoned town and reopened it for the local people. You and yours are welcome to drink and gamble here, but first you turn over them guns."

"That is funny," said Hunter, "I was thinkin' the same for you and your men."

"I heard luck runs with you gunslinger, but you are outnumbered."

At that moment the back door behind the bar opened and a double barrel poked through the gap and rested at the back of the bar keeps head making him step away from a weapon under the bar. He was directed back by Walt and Jebidiah so they could enter. The red legs pulled their pistols slow and so did Bird and Bodie. Hunter and the Colonel did not move but directed their men.

"Hold your fire."

"Take it easy, hold."

It was a small miracle that no one on either side pulled the trigger!

"The odds are a bit more even Colonel." Hunter said.

The tension was building in the room and one false move would result in a blood bath.

"Looks like what we got here is a Mexican standoff," said the Colonel, "Problem is there ain't no Mexicans here-a-bouts."

Hunter ignored the man's wit, "Why don't you and me take it to the street and spare these men? Winner gets the town."

The Colonel laughed hard and long.

"I was born at night time gunslinger, but it weren't last night."

Walt glared at the Colonel with scorn for using his saying. Hunter noticed this and almost grinned. He then realized that Helen was not with them. Hunter hardly got a chance to wonder what they were up too; when a lit stick of dynamite tied to a rock crashed through the small front window, hit a table and then went to the floor in the center of the saloon. The only two doors were covered by Hunter and his people and giving them the advantage. Everyone other than Walt and Jebidiah scrambled for the doors! Walt and Jeb began firing on the blue coats. Bodie and Bird were helping shove the locals out the front. Hunter pulled his pistol and aimed for the Colonel who had already flipped the table and ducked down behind it. Hunters 44 caliber's hit the top but the wood was thick and they did not make it through. The red legs were dropping and firing back as the lit fuse was nearing its end. The Colonel slid the table with him to the back door and rammed Walt before he could fire the shotgun and knocking him to the ground behind the bar. Jedidiah was wrestling with the big bar keep and he had managed to knock the big man out with the butt of his pistol but not before the Colonel and several of his men escaped out the back. Hunter knew he would not make the front door in time as the dynamite was out of wick so he dove over the bar and collided into Jebidiah and landing on both him and Walt.

There was only the sound of the fizzling fuse as everyone remaining in the saloon covered their heads in anticipation. With a puff of smoke the crackling sparks diminished and there was nothing but silence. The next sound was Walt's laughter. Hunter was lying on top and face to face with the old man; his breathe was brutal and Hunter moved to his feet quickly. A gun shot went off and Hunter spun with his revolver leveled in that direction only to see a red leg fall to the floor. More shots went off as the remaining crackers inside killed two remaining red Legs left behind in the saloon.

The smoke cleared and Hunter nodded a thank you to the man that may have saved his life.

"We're with yah gunslinger," said the cowboy, "them Yankees don't have no claims here."

More gun shots could be heard outside followed by the thundering hooves of horses fading away off into the distance. Stepping over bodies and overturned furniture Hunter and the men made their way to the bat wing doors leading to the street with their guns drawn. There were two dead in the street and several wounded. Around the corner came Helen riding Lady with her guns drawn. Mocha was at her side and ran to the Gunslinger. She put her front paws on his thigh; he patted her head with a gloved hand.

"Good to see yah, girl, better late than never."

Hunter looked to Helen, "Thanks for the distraction. How did you know that stick was a dud?"

"Walt told me so."

Hunter looked to Walt.

"Had a 50/50 shot," shrugged Walt, "We got lucky, again."

"I for one will take that luck whenever I can git it." Hunter replied.

They were all gathered around the porch of the saloon reloading their weapons. This battle was a victory which gave them time to take a breath but at the same time they still were on their guard.

"What's the plan now?" Bodie asked Hunter. "Do we go after them?"

"Maybe that Colonel will take what's left of his men and ride on?" Bird questioned.

"No," said Jebidiah, "that man is still fighting the war, his war, and he won't stop till his death."

"I agree," replied Hunter, "This Colonel knows nothin' but killin, and he ain't goin' nowhere."

"Well what then?" Helen asked as she dismounted Lady.

"We git this town secure and find out who's with us. Then we go after them today before they come for us." Hunter answered.

"So we again have a plan, then?" said Bird.

"That's the same damn plan as always!" Walt shouted, "But it's worked so far, what the hell?"

The James family began their work gathering supplies and mentally preparing themselves for another battle with what they considered evil men. Anyone who would attempt to steal their livelihood and kill their people would be given no quarter.

CHAPTER NINETEEN

They took an hour or so to pack their rigs for travel before meeting up at the hotel. They sat around the big dining table while Bessie was doing what she did best; serving the James Family a meal before they rode out into the backwoods. Bessie was always cooking but she had little time to prepare on this day. She still managed corn bread and swamp (palm) cabbage, Chicken fried steak and sausage gravy, hush puppies with grits, bacon and a pile of fried eggs.

They ate hardily with light conversation; once again they had that feeling of a condemned man eating his last meal. Hunter suddenly sensed trouble before the rest; with a mouthful of eggs and grits the gunslinger stood and pulled his pistol and aiming it toward the doorway. The scuffling of boots and shouting preceded the entrance of a man wearing the Red-legs, as he was thrown into the room. He hit the floor on his face, followed in by two men that Jebidiah recognized as locals; gator hunting was their living.

"What the hell is this?" shouted Walt.

The big man with long blonde hair and a beard that passed his belly answered,

"Found this Red-leg lost and stumblin' around in the marsh not far from here. Thought maybe the gunslinger might want a talk with um?"

"Son-of-a-bitch!" said the Red-leg as he got up on his hands and knees and breathing hard.

"Help him up boys and set him in that chair." Hunter said.

Bodie and Bird grabbed the man under his pits and set him forcefully in a wood chair that Jebidiah had slid in the middle of the room.

The other gator hunter was tall and slim and younger than the first. He set a revolver and two knives on the table in front of Hunter, "He's unarmed Mr. Gunslinger, and this is what he had on um."

Bessie walked into the room with a hot pot of food and when she saw the goings on she turned around and walked right back out.

Hunter holstered his revolver and pulled a chair in front of the captor and spun it around backwards before he sat. "What's your name old timer?"

"Jackson, Ron Jackson." The man said.

"I seen you in the saloon, did you shoot at my men, at me?" Hunter asked.

"I did not. I'm tired of the war and I'm tired of the killin'. I cut out the back as soon as I could."

"You got out with that Colonel." Stated Hunter, "Jeb, did you see this man fire his weapon?"

"Hell son, it happened so fast I can't be sure?"

Hunter looked around the room, "Did anyone witness this man firing on us?"

Bodie and Bird nodded no, Walt put his hands up in a questioning gesture.

"Look Sir," pleaded the man, "I don't want no trouble, I been lookin' for a way out for some time now."

Hunter paused for quite a while before he asked his next question.

"If you tell me what I need to know Mr. Jackson you might live through this day?"

"I will tell you what ever I Know." He said.

Hunter could see the surrender in the older man's face and he wanted to believe him.

"Tell me about the Colonel, who is he, what is he?"

"Colonel Charles "Doc" Jennison; he is a crazy man, he always has been. He was a Jayhawker out of Kansas and Missouri. He had been jailed by his own army for vigilantism. New politicians came to power; they released him from prison and set him up again with the Jayhawkers. He did even worse things than before. He hanged men without trial, burned homes with the families still inside, and I don't want any part of that no mores."

"What is he doing here way down in the south?" Hunter asked.

"The war is at an end and he is not needed any longer, but he can't stop, like I said, crazy."

Hunter leaned to the table and poured the man some whiskey into a tin cup. The man took it, "Thank you kindly."

"How many men does he have?" Hunter asked.

"Round twenty six give or take; we gained and lost some on the way here. You killed ten I think? "

"So roughly sixteen men left to deal with?"

The Elder Red-leg nodded yes and then sipped some more whiskey from his cup.

"Where?" Hunter continued.

"A mile or so north a here, a dry area surrounded by trees next to a small lake, this was the camp we set up before we come to town."

Hunter turned his head toward Jeb, "What do you think Jeb?"

"I think we dealt with his kind before and there all dead and we're still standin'."

Hunter looked to his left toward Bodie "Bode?"

"The Montgomery's were as crazy as they come and we handled it."

"Montgomery's?" questioned the red-leg Jackson.

"Say what?" questioned Hunter, diverting his attention to Jackson.

"James Montgomery headed up the Jayhawkers for a time. The Colonel had rode with him and they were good friends, like brothers."

Walt scoffed and shook his head, "Are you shittin' me! James Montgomery! The father of Richard and Duke and that Bitch Jane, I'm gittin' too old for this sh..."

Jebidiah cut Walt off before he could finish, "Here we go again! Now we know another reason why that Colonel is here, he ain't just runnin' from his past but he's targetin' a new enemy, us."

Helen gasped; "Oh my God" was all she could muster.

Bird took a few steps forward and bent down; and got right into the red-legs face, "Well guess what, we'll just kill all them sons-a-bitches just like we did the Montgomery's!"

The James family could not believe that the Montgomery family was still creeping up into their lives. They would have to defend their selves once again, kill or be killed was the same old story.

The room got loud as they were complaining and talking about their plight. The man Jackson leaned in toward Hunter and spoke to him personally. Hunter shook his head with concern.

"Quiet down ya'll," Hunter shouted.

They all stopped talking and gave Hunter their attention.

"The sixteen men we can most likely handle on a regular day; but Mr. Jackson here says they hold a Gatlin gun."

The look of concern was clear on everyone's face. A strange sound escaped Walt's lips and they all turned and looked at him expecting to hear his famous line "I'm gettin' too old for this shit" but it did not come. Walt looked back at all of them with his mouth open but silent. For the first time that anyone could remember Walt was speechless. This news did not sit well with anyone in the room.

"I know I've said this before always on deaf ears," Hunter said, "we can move on, head south and start a new?"

"Run?" Bird asked, "I know I'm young and full of beans but that's the coward's way out."

"I would not use the word coward," Said Bodie with a stern look at the boy, "but if we run this Yank won't give it up, he will follow and hunt us down."

Hunter looked to Helen who was pacing in deep thought. He then looked to Jebidiah.

"Bodie's right, I seen these types all my life, Jayhawker's don't give it up."

"Walt?" Hunter asked.

Walt just raised a hand, and took a bottle from the table top and kicked it back. Helen walked over to Walt's side and reached out for his bottle. He handed it over and she took a swig. All eyes were upon her: she took another draw from the bottle before her speech.

"We have fought and killed for this town so many times, we rebuilt it again and again. I ain't givin' her up now. This time little James goes with Bessie and hidden well, no Injuns, I ain't goin' through that again."

"It's settled then, "said Hunter, "six against sixteen and a Gatlin Gun."

"Seven" said Ron Jackson, "If you'll have me?"

No one objected, so Hunter agreed. "You are welcomed to fight with us Mr. Jackson but if your intentions are anythin' different than what you say, I will kill you."

"Yes sir," said Jackson, "I have no where's to go. You people are the most honorable I have been around in some time."

Hunter returned the man's revolver and knives to him. Jackson thanked him with a nod.

"Bird" said Hunter as he directed his eyes.

Bird walked to a table against the wall and grabbed a rifle and a box of ammo. He brought it to the man named Jackson and handed it to him. Bird gave him a warning look before walking away.

Once again the James Family, plus one, prepared for battle. They were going up against a crazy man with some serious fire power. Hunter had somewhat of a plan but he kept it to himself for now. Depending on where and when they found the enemy would he decide the next course of action?

Chapter Twenty

They traveled under the cover of darkness with Hunter and Jackson leading the way. The old man turned out to be a good woodsman and brought them straight to a small clearing outside the camp of his former Colonel; the clearing was on high ground and located at a safe distance from detection. Hunter grabbed the bottom branch of an oak tree and slung himself up. He extended the scope and surveyed the area. In his circular view he could see four military tents illuminated by the fire light. Their horses were outfitted with pads and tied to a line just outside the camp. The saddles were next to each animal for a quick dress. Just outside the fire light was a horse hooked to a covered wagon; this was clearly the Gatlin gun. There were two armed men on watch walking the perimeter as the others slept.

Hunter jumped down from his perch and went to Zeke's side where he removed his bow and quiver that held five arrows.

Walt could not contain himself, "Well what the hell did you see with that glass son?

"Two guards on the watch and the rest is quiet."

"What's the plan Hunter?" Helen asked.

"I will take out the guards with the arrows, if I hit my marks they will fall without alerting the others. If not, well? Jebidiah I need you to go for the big gun with that dynamite as soon as the guards are down, use single sticks so you don't blow us all up."

"I got it," replied Jebidiah, "but what if I can get there and pull that horse and wagon to the perimeter, I can then use the gun against the Yanks."

"OOH doggy," said Walt, "I like that idear best. If you can get a hold of that gun it would go a long ways to even up the odds. Bring that baby home afterwards; build a tower for it in the protection of Myakka City?"

"I git yah Walt," said Hunter, "but the aim is not to let one red leg get to that gun or they could take us all out, that needs to be the first thought. Now, let us move while we have the night."

All the men and Helen began to move into their positions. Hunter went in first to take out the two guards on the night watch. The man named Jackson would have to be trusted and hopes that he were not a traitor twice in one day.

Hunter used his skills of his child hood and the Indian blood that ran through his veins to silently move through the forest. He settled in behind an oak tree and drew back the bow string with an arrow loaded. Hunter could see both men on either side of the perimeter, one on the left of him and one on the right. He decided the man on his left would go first as he was further away from the tents that held the sleeping men. With careful aim and a loose, the arrow hit its mark into the throat of the walking guard. A gurgle was all the man could voice as he fell to his knees and then face first into the dirt. With another arrow loaded Hunter swung to his right; he took aim for the neck of the second guard who was walking his route. Suddenly he stepped off the perimeter and a tree blocked Hunters shot. Into the woods went the man on watch. Hunter held the bow string and observed; he had lost sight of the guard.

The man must have heard something and went to investigate or he was relieving himself, this was Hunters thought. The guard's actions were throwing off the timing of Hunters crew. If they came in early from their positions it could be disastrous.

Hunter lowered the bow and arrow using both eyes to see. After a short moment the guard appeared into the clearing with his head down and tying his britches. Hunter raised the bow and arrow and took aim with one eye shut. The Red leg was facing the gunslinger and standing perfectly still and concentrating on his crotch area. Hunter aimed at the top of his hat; the man finished and then raised his head putting his Adams apple in Hunters line of sight. He loosed the arrow right when the red leg picked up his right foot to begin walking. His boot hovered over the ground as the man grabbed at his throat with the arrow; he had the look of confusion on his face. He went straight back and disappeared into the woods with a fall.

All was quiet; Hunter met Jebidiah at the Gatling gun and stopped him from blowing it up. Instead he directed him into the seat of the wagon to ride out with the big gun. Hunter grabbed a lit torch and nodded to Jebidiah, "Ayah, Ayah" Jeb yelled.

Hunter threw the torch at the closest tent and set it ablaze. Men came scrambling out, dressing while stumbling and shooting. The gunslinger pulled his pistols and took down two men. Walt appeared out of the darkness to his side and took out a third with the shotgun. Yankee soldiers with the red legs poured out of the other tents firing in Hunter and Walt's direction, the gunslinger and the old man fired back. Bodie, Bird and Helen out flanked them and began firing, killing more of the unexpected soldiers. Hunter and Walt fanned out and concentrated their fire on another tent; like shooting fish in a barrel. The red leg soldiers were caught sleeping and completely off their guard. The plan had seemed to work perfectly. Jebidiah had ridden away with the Gatling gun and all the bad men were being killed one by one.

The tent that was on fire had burned away and luckily did not spread into the woods. Hunter and Walt went from tent to tent while Helen, Bodie and Bird followed and covered them.

Hunter looked around, "Where is Jackson?"

No one answered at first, then Walt spoke up, "Not only Jackson but where is that crazy ass Colonel?

Hunter quickly went to the perimeter where the horses were tied. They had finally calmed down from the fire and shooting. Two horses were missing and the tracks showed they had headed for the road.

"They are going after Jeb and the gun, the traitor Jackson and the Colonel."

"I got it said Bird."

"No!" said Hunter, "I want the man named Jackson, and Zeke is the fastest horse here. Burn everything and then follow." And then Hunter was gone before Helen or anyone could argue.

Bodie and Bird, Walt and Helen drug the tents over the top of the camp fire. They released the horses and piled the saddles and gear in the growing flames to burn.

Helen yelled through the rising smoke, "Bodie! You and Bird go after Hunter; Walt can help me finish up here."

Bodie nodded and signaled to Bird. They ran to their mounts; they grabbed Jebidiah's horse and let out at a run. Walt and Helen would finish up quickly and then soon follow.

Chapter Twenty-One

As the battle began, Jebidiah had ridden out quickly at full speed with the two horse team and the wagon carrying the Gatlin Gun. Now that he was at a safe distance from the fight he slowed and headed for Myakka City. Jebidiah was worried about his horse that he was forced to leave behind. He suddenly pulled back on the reins bringing the horse to a stop. He stood up off the wagon seat and strained to look down the road; over the tree tops Jebidiah could see smoke but could not hear any gun fire. He was not sure what to do? He was convinced his friends had prevailed for they had the Half-breed gunslinger at their side.

He listened intently and heard nothing at the first; but soon he did feel something that was not quite right. Jebidiah stepped over the seat and grabbed the big gun. The magazine was loaded and there was a box full at his feet. The barrel was aimed out the back of the wagon and with his hand on the crank he waited.

Suddenly the sounds of horses moving fast down the dirt road could be heard. There was a turn covered by trees 200 feet back; Jebidiah told himself to wait and see who was coming around the corner before he fired. He did not want to shoot his own people. Around the corner came the crazy Colonel and the liar named Jackson. Jebidiah turned the crank on the big gun and it came alive with a bang. Smoke and gases filled the air. Four of the large bullets hit the ground in front of the two men as they reared up their horses. The gun spooked the horses that were attached to his wagon and they took off at a run almost throwing Jebidiah out the back. Not only was Jebidiah hanging on for dear life but the two men were chasing him now and firing at him. Bullets whizzed by his head and the wagon was out of his control and at times barely touching the road. Jebidiah was hanging on to the back of the wooden bench seat for dear life as bullets splintered off pieces of lumber from the wagon. A sharp turn came into Jebidiah's view up ahead and he made a split second decision to jump into the ditch on the left before the right turn as the men were gaining on the wagon.

Walt's voice sprang into the thoughts of Jebidiah's head; "I'm too old for this shit!"

As soon as the wagon turned out of the view of his pursuer's Jebidiah grabbed his rifle and jumped from the wagon. He aimed for the bank of the ditch preparing to tuck and roll down and into the shallow waters below. He hit the sandy bank; He rolled and rolled six times and then hit the water with a splash, soaking his right side. Before he jumped he made a conscience decision to hold on to his rifle at all cost and he was able to do so. The horses continued on down the road with the big gun in tow leaving Jebidiah behind. Jebidiah began his climb up the bank cussing and groaning. He made it to the top of the bank where he could see down the road. He cocked his rifle to shoot the men from the ground level and using the ditch for cover, but they were already gone as they chased down the wagon.

"Shit!" Jebidiah cursed.

He laid their breathing hard, pissed at himself for losing the big gun.

Few minutes went by when Jebidiah heard hooves coming down the road; he turned his head to see the Gunslinger and Zeke coming fast. He tried to get to his feet from the bank to wave them down, but he lost his footing in the loose sand and rolled down the ditch. He did not stop until he hit the bottom with another splash, this time landing on his left side. He pulled himself up out of the shallow water.

"Son-of-a-Bitch!" yelled Jebidiah. There was not a dry spot left on his clothes. He was soaked to the bone. Again, he dragged himself up the bank, out of the ditch and on to the road; Jebidiah began walking while cleaning sand and water from the chamber of his rifle. He checked his pistol next; it was cleaner and dryer than the Winchester long gun.

"Son-of-a-Bitch!" again cursed Jebidiah, when he realized he had lost his hat. He looked back toward the ditch: "Hell no!" he would not negotiate the steep bank, not even for his hat. Jebidiah would miss his old hat but right now he was missing his horse even more.

Jebidiah had walked for about ten minutes following the tracks on the road left by the wagon when he heard horses coming from behind him, and they were coming fast. He cocked his rifle as he turned and raised it to his shoulder for his aim, with his finger pressing against the trigger. He immediately rested his digit and lowered the long gun with a smile as Bodie and Bird thundered to his position then pulled back on the reins. The dust kicked up and covered Jebidiah's wet cloths.

"Really!" Jebidiah said with disgust, "Can't you see I just had my bath?"

Bird was smiling from ear to ear at the looks of the old man.

"You be lookin' for a horse?" asked Bodie with a grin, as he held out the reins to Jebidiah's horse.

"Come on down here Bode and I'll give you a big sloppy kiss." Jebidiah replied.

"Save them kisses for your horse there grandpa."

Jebidiah slid his rifle into the saddles scabbard and mounted his Cracker horse. Bird turned his horse around and came along side Jebidiah and produced his hat from behind his back.

"Thank you much." Jebidiah said with a smile. "I never thought I would ever see this old Brim again?" He was pleased that the hat was dry as he capped his head drawing the string under his chin.

"Anythin' is better than lookin' at your huge white forehead." Bird joked.

"The Gatlin Gun?" asked Bodie.

"A run away,' replied Jeb, "The Colonel and Jackson are after it with Hunter right on their tail."

"What do you say we give the gunslinger a hand?" suggested Bodie.

With nods all around the men rode hard down the road in the direction that headed back to Myakka City.

Chapter Twenty-Two

Hunter turned a corner at full speed and saw a flash of the two men just before they turned another corner up the road. He came to that corner and turned to see them turn another corner. They were much closer this time. Hunter was gaining fast. He turned another corner on to a good half mile straight away where he saw the men and the run-away wagon. He put the spurs to Zeke and found more speed. The two men were gaining on the horses and wagon that carried the Gatlin gun. Hunter must get in firing range before they could stop the wagon and turn the big gun on him. At a full run Hunter locked his legs in the saddle and slid his rifle from its sheath. There was no steading his aim but with the end of the barrel moving in a circular motion he would fire at the mid back of the man called Jackson. He pulled the trigger and it hit the man in the shoulder but, he jerked and looked back but did not fall. The second shot missed him completely but his horse was slowing down as Hunter gained. Jackson stopped his horse and turned toward Hunter. He pulled his pistol while Hunter had cocked his rifle one handed and they both fired. Jackson missed and Hunters bullet caught Jackson in the side of the mouth shattering his cheek bone with the large caliber. The Colonel saw Jackson disappear from the corner of his eye; He turned his head to see Jacksons face open up with a splash of blood and bone as he fell to the ground. The gunfire had accelerated the speed of the horses pulling the wagon. The Colonel new he must turn and fight or die with a bullet in his back. The Gunslinger was closing fast; the Colonel slowed and turned his horse, giving up the pursuit of the wagon, he pulled a pistol and charged. Hunter had sheathed his rifle and pulled his pistol. The two men were closing on each other fast and at twenty feet the Colonel fired aiming and hitting Zeke in the chest, putting down the Appaloosa making Hunter miss with his shot. The gunslinger and his horses went down as one. The Colonel past them and turned. Hunter had barrel rolled and came to his feet losing the revolver in his hand. Anger quickly grew inside him, for he knew the killing of his horse was an intentional strategy. The Colonel fired and missed; Hunter pulled his left handed pistol and began walking forward towards the Colonel with purpose; with the palm of his hand he slammed the hammer unloading the 45. Bullets 3, 4, and 6 hit the Colonel in his chest, shoulder and neck throwing him backwards from his horse and to the ground where he lay still. Hunter ran back quickly to Zeke and knelt down. The Appaloosa was lifeless; the shot hit the heart killing him instantly. Hunter sighed and lowered his head, anger and sadness overwhelmed him. If he were the type of man capable of crying he would have done it now. He looked toward the Colonel who was still motionless. He collected his other pistol and holstered it. He walked to where the Colonel lay loading the empty 45 as he went. Hunter stood over the dead man and had to calm himself or unload his revolver into his lifeless body. Instead he kicked the body three times the next harder than the first, "You Son-of-a-Bitch!" He yelled loudly.

Hunters head was buzzing and he did not hear the horses closing in on him as he walked back over to his departed appaloosa. It was Bodie, Bird and Jebidiah; they had collected the Colonels horse from down the road and brought it back with them. The three men felt sadness as they looked upon Zeke, for they knew what it was like to lose a good horse. The times over many years that Zeke and Hunter had ridden together were something more. No one said a word for the looks on their faces said it all.

Hunter took the reins of the Colonel's horse and dropped the rig from its back. He walked the grey to where Zeke lie. Bird had jumped down from his mount and helped Hunter remove the saddle from the Zeke's back. When done, Hunter nodded thanks to Bird.

"Helen? Walt?" Hunter asked.

"Should be right behind us? Just down the road a spell." Jebidiah answered.

"You three go for the wagon, with no one chasing it them horses should slow to a stop." said Hunter "Take the gun to Myakka City; I'm goin' back for Walt and Helen. I don't want any more losses today."

They cleared the road by sliding the bodies into the ditches for the gators to feed. When it came time to deal with the horse Jebidiah spoke up, "We got this son, you go on." Hunter mounted and left, heading back the way they had come. The boys hooked the appaloosa up to ropes and dragged his body along the bank until the horse hit the slope and began to slide. They cut the ropes and Zeke slid then rolled once into the water. Bird stared down at the Gunslingers horse for a moment and then went to mount his own. He rubbed his horse's neck affectionately feeling lucky they both lived at this moment.

Jebidiah, Bodie and Bird moved out at a run to chase down the Gatling gun before someone more murderous than they might find it. In the wrong hands fire power like that gun could start another war. There were still packs of renegade Indians in the swamps hell bent on running the white men out of these lands, and with a gun of that sort they could do much damage.

It did not take long for the men to run down the wagon as the horses were tired and found grazing on the side of the road. Bird tied his horse to the wagon and then took the reins from the bench seat. Myakka City was not too far and they would walk the horses the rest of the way.

Hunter rode hard and was getting use to his new horse. It was a good breed and still had some youth. Hunter would not name this horse or any other ever again for it hurt too much to lose an animal with a name.

Hunter caught up with Helen and Walt a few miles down the road and meeting them head on. They talked briefly; Hunter shook his head when asked about Zeke. Both knew what it was like to lose a good horse and moving forward with the next animal was the only thing one could do. Out in the West and up North sometimes men were forced to eat their horses for meat, but in the swamps of Florida there were plenty of game, crops and fish. No men in these parts were forced to eat their own horses to survive a harsh winter or lifeless desert.

Hunter, Helen and Walt moved out with purpose to help their friends in the pursuit of the Gatling gun. The tracks were easy to follow on the road that led into Myakka City; of course they did not need tracks to find home.

They arrived before sundown to find their friends in Mat's Saloon drinking and eating quietly. Walt had thrown the few patrons from the bar and closed up for what he called a private get-together. Bessie served food and then was invited to join them at the tables. Mocha gave licks to all and begged for table scraps, wagging her tail constantly. Little James laughed and chased the dog around after Helen finally released him from her grasp. Beer and whiskey flowed till the late hour, everyone was glad to be home and alive.

Chapter Twenty-Three

The year was 1868, three years after the end of the American Civil War. The first Florida Governor was elected with black men voting for the first time in the nation's history. To bring the states together pardons were issued for crimes committed during the war and after. This included The Half-Breed Gunslinger named Hunter James Dolin.

Since the ending of the war in 1865 there had been a flux of Northerners exploring lands all across the country. The great Florida land rush was in full swing, mostly due to Harriet Beecher Stowe. Her columns in her brother Henrys New York newspaper, *The Christian Union,* Brought many travelers. The Myakka River Valley came to be known as Paradise for hunting and fishing. Out of state hunters were attracted to the area by the abundance of game. Cattle Barons were many and citrus and sugar cane farmers flourished. Times were changing quickly all across the country and Florida's beauty and warm weather attracted many.

Jebidiah had passed shortly after the last battle of Myakka and like an old married couple Walt soon followed; their hearts not able to function any longer. These were honorable men in the end and lived longer than they should have in these times. Bodie and Bird took over the town running the Hotel and Mats Saloon. People came far and wide to eat the cooking's of Miss Bessie. She had become a celebrity after an article had been written in a New York newspaper.

Hunter, Helen, little James and Mocha moved back out to the Dolin cabin. They fished and grew vegetables and Hunter took to tracking for hire. He quickly became one of the most sought out hunting guides in the area for rich northerners and Englishmen from across the pond. For a price he would occasionally autograph a wanted poster with his likeness and show off his quick draw skills.

Life had changed quickly for the James Family and these are the last writings of the legend of the southern swamps of Florida. The last writings of the life and times of Hunter James Dolin known as The Half-Breed Gunslinger, as written,

By, Little James Dolin.

The End

ABOUT THE AUTHOR

Bret Lee Hart, a second generation Floridian, has spent the last twenty-five years in Marine construction; he is married and the father of two. His mother's maiden name is Emerson, as in Ralph Waldo, and on his father's side, Edgar Allen Poe can be found hanging on the family tree. With this bloodline of writers, and being named after Bret Harte from his western short stories, it was inevitable his imagination would find its way into print.

The *Half-Breed Gunslinger, Hunter James Dolin (Book II), Montgomery's Revenge (Book III), Wanted Dead (Book IV),* and *Wars End (Book V)* are the five books in this "cracker Western" series, as Bret calls them, and are available at major online book retailers.

The Fangslinger and the Preacher, Preacher Jack and the Fangslinger (Book II) are also available with many other adventures soon to be unleashed from this exciting storyteller's mind in various genres, including Fantasy and the Paranormal.

Follow Bret Lee Hart on Facebook:
https://facebook.com/bretleehart

OTHER WORKS AVAILABLE FROM
BRET LEE HART

✳ ✳ ✳ ✳ ✳

~ A Western action adventure, the first in
"The Half-Breed Gunslinger" *series ~*

In 1860 there was more open range cattle in Florida than in Texas and all the other states combined. It took a special breed of man to live there, and an even harder man to survive. Hunter James Dolin, half white and half Indian, was such a man. He was a gambler by trade and a gunslinger of necessity and attracted trouble wherever he traveled. But with his two Colt Walkers and bowie knife, he could handle almost anything.

Brief excerpt:
About ninety miles back and a few days earlier, in the crackerjack Saloon along the Withlacoochee River, Dolin's ace-high straight flush had beat one of the three outlaws' full house. He won fair and square – two ounces of gold and a just 'broke in' Henry rifle. These days that was more than reason enough to kill a man.

Hunter had felt the itch in his craw that warned him he'd out-stayed his welcome, and knew it was high time for him to leave this place. Without taking his eyes off the men at the poker table, Hunter had gathered up his winnings, while he spoke, "Thank you, Gentlemen. It's been a pleasure."

The man at the table to Hunter's left, the one who just lost his Henry rifle, had stood and replied angrily, "Do you think we're just gonna let you walk on out of here, half-breed?"

✳ ✳ ✳ ✳ ✳

Spurred by revenge...
Gunfights and gold...
One man against the odds...

Hunter James Dolin survived the revenge war of Myakka City, Florida, by killing the men who raised their guns against him and his loved ones – all but one.

The Governor directed the Army to investigate, forcing the Half-Breed Gunslinger to seek refuge deep in the swamps of the Everglades.

Hunter James Dolin was content to live the rest of his life in solitude – 'til he was sought out and told of the whereabouts of the one that got away.

This would spark a new battle of revenge, overshadowed by the Civil War, but not soon forgotten by the people who inhabit the Florida swamplands.

Brief excerpt:

Scooter was swinging like a pendulum as very large Gators came up out of the water and snapped at the chicken, just out of reach of the man's head. Scooter was screaming again, as Hunter backed Zeke up a bit, putting his face and head closer to the teeth-laden jaws of the twelve-foot reptiles. The largest of the Gators stretched his neck up and snapped two pieces of chicken hanging down less than a foot from Scooter Johnson's head.

"PULL ME UP!!!! PULL ME UP!!!!" shrieked the dangling man. "I'm not the last – Montgomery's alive! *HE'S ALIVE, PLEASE!!!"*

Hunter urged the Appaloosa forward so the rope hanging over the branch moved with him, pulling Scooter up and out of reach of the Gator's bite.

"What do you mean, *he's alive?"* yelled Hunter. "I blowed him up in his own hotel."

✳ ✳ ✳ ✳ ✳

~ A Western action adventure, the third in "The Half-Breed Gunslinger" series, set in Florida. Author Bret Lee Hart reminds us his state was once as wild as the West – and just as deadly. ~

Duke Montgomery is an Indian fighter – a hard-as-nails killer, plain and simple – who doesn't think twice about ambushing a man or killing him face-to-face. When he learns his brother Richard is dead, killed by the Half-Breed Gunslinger, Duke goes on the hunt.

To avoid trouble after his dealings with Richard Montgomery, Hunter James Dolin and the woman, Helen, travel deep into the Everglades to live in peace for a while. But, as is the way of the world, trouble soon comes looking for them.

How many will die as Montgomery seeks the Half-Breed Gunslinger to get revenge? And what surprises are in store for Hunter James Dolin?

Brief Excerpt:
"Where you headed, mister?" asked Billy.

"Myakka City is my first stop," replied Duke.

"Where's that at, Billy?" whispered Junior, leaning toward Billy.

"Not sure," said Billy, "Where's that city at, Mister? Maybe we could tag along with yah?"

There it was; Duke had just recruited these two easily with his larger mind. He grabbed the whiskey bottle by its neck, and with the other hand chugged the last of his beer then slammed the glass mug on the counter. "We leave tomorrow mornin' at sunup, meet me at the hotel. You will be paid if you do your jobs and don't git yourself killed." Duke turned and headed for the door, taking his whiskey bottle with him.

"What might our jobs be?" said Billy to his back.

The shirtless, scarred, muscle man stopped and turned after two steps. "We're going to Florida to kill a stinkin' half-breed."

Billy and Junior looked at one another and grinned with confidence that the job would be easy enough.

"What do your friends call you, Mister?" Junior asked.

"I don't have any friends, but you will call me Sir." Duke turned and walked out, leaving the saloon doors swinging behind him.

* * * * *

~ A Western action adventure, the forth in
"The Half-Breed Gunslinger" series, set in Florida.

While *The Half-Breed Gunslinger* fights for his life against infection from a gunshot wound, there are wanted posters being printed with his name and likeness. A $5,000 bounty on the head of Hunter James Dolin is more than enough money to attract men to the swamps of south Florida. The ending of the Civil War turns soldiers into bounty hunters as the North feels the need to cleanse the South, and men find ways to make a living.

The gunslinger's woman carries his child; Helen will need help from their close friends as her pregnancy progresses. Jebidiah and Walt will protect Helen at all costs with their experience and grit. Bodie and Bird, with their own skills, will be by their side in whatever comes their way. To their surprise, unexpected rivals come after the newly named Dolin Family.

Brief excerpt:
"What's goin' on, Hunter? Talk to me."

"Bounty hunter keeping track of our whereabouts." Helen's hand went to the butt of her gun. "Easy, woman; he's gone for now, but he will be back and with friends."

"What will we do?" she asked calmly.

"We can't stay here, it's too open. We could hold them off inside the cabin but for only so long; eventually they would burn us out. Myakka City is where our friends are; they will increase our numbers."

"Then we'll git little James, Alameda and Mocha and go to town at once."

"It ain't safe for the boy or you. I think maybe you should take little James and go with Alameda to the Seminole tribe lands..." Before he could finish, Helen was on her feet and shaking her head.

"I will not stay with that Sam Jones; Alameda can take little James and Mocha out there but I will go where you go." She turned and began walking up the bank to the cabin. "We best git packin'."

Hunter knew Helen meant to stand firm on her decision and there was nothing he could say to change her mind once she had made it. The boy would be safest with the tribe and Helen's skill with the gun would be handy. She had been battle tested and had killed without prejudice. She would be more dangerous now that she was a mother, like a mamma bear protecting her cub.

✳ ✳ ✳ ✳ ✳

~ *A Western action adventure, the fifth in*
"The Half-Breed Gunslinger" *series, set in Florida.*

The three year Montgomery/ Dolin War was over, and not one family member named Montgomery was left alive. Hunter James Dolin had killed Richard Montgomery, his brother Duke Montgomery and their sister Jane Montgomery. The next man in line named Little Owl, for Chief of the Snake Clan of the Miccosukee, of the Seminole Indian Tribe was killed by the hand of the Half-Breed Gunslinger. Little Owl and his loyal braves were no more.

Myakka City and the James family had survived the last battle and Helen and little James were found alive at the waters' edge. Their current enemies were dead but Hunter was concerned about the wanted posters. There was no way to know how many had been printed and how far they had spread? The authors of the prints were dead but it would take time for this to be known and then believed. Five thousand dollars was a world of money and there would be men coming to kill the Half-breed Gunslinger and seeking their fortune.

Brief excerpt:
"The knife," said Hooker.

Hunter reached back and pulled the bowie from the sheath that was clipped to his pants at his back. Daryl took that too, with the same grin, only bigger.

"You take good care of that, Daryl; I will be needin' that back."

The stare of the gunslinger's steel blue eyes froze Daryl for a moment. His smile faded and then came back, but only a little.

"Oh, you won't need this no more, half-breed, not where you goin'."

"Daryl! I'm only gonna tell yah one more time to shut the hell up," the Captain warned. "Jimbo, tie his hands in the front; he's got to ride."

The big mouth drover picked up Hunter's pistol belt from the floor as Jimbo escorted the gunslinger outside. Zeke was there, and Hunter was placed on his back by two of the men.

"Where we headed, Captain?" Hunter asked.

"Daryl and Jimbo here will take you to Fort Foster and we'll let the army decide your fate."

"What of my family, Captain?" Hunter asked.

"When they are ready for travel I will personally escort them wherever they would like to go, unharmed. I give you my word as a lawman and a gentleman."

"You do as you say, Captain, and I will allow you to live. I give you my word, but your men here, a pass will not be givin'."

Jimbo glared at Hunter and Daryl laughed out loud.

"Let's go, tough guy," Jimbo replied.

"You try anythin', half-breed, and I'll kill yah with your own guns," Daryl said while resting his hand on Hunter's 44s that he now wore on his hip.

Hunter was glad to see his bowie knife tucked in the man's belt for he would need it as well on his return.

* * * * *

~ A Paranormal Western based on the
age-old battle of good versus evil ~

Master Andelko Balas is the leader of a bored, and therefore troublesome, vampire coven in Romania in the 1880s. Colonel Richard Andersson brings relief to the boredom by discovering tales of the American West and setting the coven on an exciting, but bloody, journey to a new land.

Jack Denton, reformed gunfighter, former preacher, now a drunkard, has visions of a great evil coming to Arizona as he wanders in the desert. Then he meets an Indian Chief and is given a silver sword, a special cross, and a mission. Jack is led to Black Mountain Mesa where an unusual storm is brewing and he has to face the greatest battle of his life.

Is this the last battle for the world as he knows it? Will his renewed faith and special weapons be enough to defeat such evil?

Brief Excerpt:
Black Mesa Mountain, Arizona, 1885
He went by the name Preacher Jack, given to him by his small congregation in New Mexico. He had buried the name Anderson in the past, going by the name Jack Denton in fear of being discovered by the law, or the lawless. It was a simple life he now led, and a good life for Preacher Jack, until God's plan for him continued forward. When his wife and daughter died from disease that swept through the small Mexican village, Jack lost his faith in God and left New Mexico, wandering aimlessly, not caring if he lived or died. Forty-year-old Jack Denton, a fallen preacher, was now a faithless drunkard living off whiskey – his only thoughts were of drinking himself to death.

Forty days and forty nights into his journey of despair, Jack found refuge in an abandoned mining shack to get some rest. A vision appeared to him as he slept, the drunken haze in which he slumbered left him, allowing the vivid images of his dream to come forth...

Fear overwhelmed him as something that Jack could only describe as a demon straight from hell swooped down on top of him, baring bloody fangs to devour his flesh.

Jack Denton awoke with a scream from the dirt floor of the mining shack.

* * * * *

~ The Paranormal Western sequel to
"The Fangslinger and the Preacher" ~

Preacher Jack and his comrade Richard, a centuries-old Romanian soldier, thought their battle against evil was won after their climactic battle with the master vampire Andelko Balas at the top of Black Mountain Mesa. But Richard's former master was not vanquished permanently; the Fallen One has raised him up, and now Balas has an undead army at his command. The Preacher and the Fangslinger, aided by the mystical Indian White Owl and his followers, are now all that stands in the way of the vampire master's plan to empower his dark lord and unleash hell on earth.

Will the Preacher's faith be strong enough to sustain them?

Brief Excerpt:

On his return to camp, Jack was surprised to see that Richard had pulled himself up and was now leaning against a flat rock formation alongside the campsite that partially blocked the dry desert wind. As Jack got closer he could see that the color in Richard's face was much better. Jack then realized that the colonel had positioned himself in a shady spot to avoid the rays of the morning light. This concerned the Preacher, for this was something a man with the blood of a vampire might do.

"Does the sun bother you?" Jack asked.

"Slightly, yes," answered Richard, "may I bother you for some additional water?"

Jack fetched the canteen and went to one knee as he handed it over, but this time Jack did so at a greater distance.

Richard took several small sips, and then the two men stared at one another for a moment.

"You do not trust me so?"

"Ain't sure just yet," answered Jack, "you did save my life on that mountain, and the rumor is that we are kin, but the simple fact that you're hidin' from the sun does got me wonderin'."

www.ingramcontent.com/pod-product-compliance
Lightning Source LLC
Chambersburg PA
CBHW061303120726

48001CB00001B/455